STUNNING T

ff

STUNNING THE PUNTERS

Robert Sproat

faber and faber

LONDON · BOSTON

First published in 1986 by
Faber and Faber Limited
3 Queen Square London WC1N 3AU

Filmset by Goodfellow & Egan Ltd
Cambridge
Printed in Great Britain by
Redwood Burn Ltd
Trowbridge Wiltshire
All rights reserved

© Robert Sproat 1986

'Almost Graceful like a Dancer' was first
published in the *New Statesman* and
'Stunning the Punters' in *The Fiction Magazine*

British Library Cataloguing in Publication Data

Sproat, Robert
Stunning the punters
I. Title
823'.914[F]   PR6069.P7/
ISBN 0-571-13823-3

CONTENTS

'London, thou art the flour of Cities all.'

William Dunbar, Scotch Toady

'Carry on, boys, and continue like hell.'

G. V. Desani, *All About H. Hatterr*

BLACK MADONNA
TWO-WHEEL GYPSY QUEEN

For Hilary Holden and Tony Prime

Some things look right as rain, but when you think about them it don't stand up, right? Like just over the way there it's these Peabody Trust flats. Hundreds of years old and four floors high and no lifts. And they all got these outside balconies with the painted iron railings and they always got washing out to dry on the balconies. There's a waiting queue of hundreds of years to get one of them flats because they fix the rent so low and they only give it to you if you're a problem family. I go past these flats nearly every day and I see where there's one place on the fourth floor always got a push-bike out on the balcony. Proper drop-handle racing job with ten-speed gears and no mudguards. Looks good. I get so I look for it special every time I go past, right? It's like a good luck thing to see it there. You feel good because it looks so right sitting there on the balcony, so sort of *natural*, you know? But then when you think of the walk up four flights of stairs . . .

Right?

Martin, that's my dad, all my life he's been Bike Man. That's motor bikes; I never seen him with a push-bike. Right now I bet he's out in the garage working on that stinky old Squariel he's been trying to get sorted since I was in the second year, and I'm leaving in June. When Wayne or Sean come round for me, though, he won't talk to them about bikes and he just goes and shuts himself away with his old wreck till they've gone. Or else he's been on the piss and he gives them the verbals about their bikes and tells them stuff like Japcrap and Suzuki Tawdry which is out of order and Wayne says he's going to do Martin. Only I told him he can't or I

11

won't go with him no more. Plus he is scared of Eric. Eric is my brother and not friendly and don't never say nothing only 'Bollocks' and 'Rat off'. Martin says where it's just a phrase he's going through. Eric don't like bikers, though, and Wayne is scared of him. Martin would like to stop me going with Sean and Wayne but Eric don't care so long as they leave him out of it. Martin can't stop me, though. Like when he first seen me in my leather mini in the garden of the Albion and he was pissed up and he starts screaming at me in front of everybody to cover myself up, I just tell him to fuck off, Martin, and if you got it, flaunt it, right? And he can't do nothing about it due to he's scared of Eric too. I lip him straight back, Martin. Same as in school. If any teacher say anything to me, I lip them straight back until they let me be. If everybody's a bit of a bastard, you got to be a bit of a bastard back at them, right?

Wayne and Sean was the first boys I ever brung back to the house and I thought Martin would be their friend on account of being Bike Man. I mean, you'd think he could have a really sort of *interesting* conversation with them over the bikes, plus Martin in a talking mood is world long-distance rabbiting champion. But he just sits there and grunts at them like he always does on one of those days when you can see where Eric gets it from, and Sean and Wayne think he's getting at them and they take me aside and say 'Sod this' and leave. You can't blame them really except maybe Wayne a bit, because he always thinks everybody's getting at him and he give away his Walkman due to the people across the street talking about him every time he turns the volume up.

And after they've gone, Martin goes, 'Good Christ, Mandy, where do you find them; they look like something out of Damon Rudyard,' and I don't really get what he's driving at but you can't mistake that *tone*, right? So I do my pieces and I tell him he's no fucking oil painting himself and quite a lot of other stuff besides until Martin goes slamming off into his garage and I go in the bog and throw up.

12

When he's in a talking mood, Martin is always saying things where I can't see what he's driving at and that's a reason I stopped really listening to him. I think Eric can see what he's driving at, but Eric don't listen to him no more either. Eric can talk even better than Martin when he wants to but most of the time he don't want to. He says Martin talks like that due to where his brains have been unbalanced by too much education and now everything in the world makes him unhappy when he thinks about it. Sometimes I don't get what Eric is driving at either, but he has got A-levels, right?

Eric is a great disappointment to Martin. He wants Eric to go to college like he done but Eric says it is a load of bollocks and he won't do it. He says to look what it done for Martin, right? Plus he says nowadays it don't even get you any sort of a job so what's the point? Eric says he reckons too much education is like polishing a piece of metal. First of all you take off the rough, then you give it a bit of a shine, then it gets like a mirror and dazzles you, and if you keep on going you wear it away to where it won't stand a knock, and he ain't going to be that piece of metal, right? But most of the time Eric don't say nothing only 'Bollocks' and 'Bog off'.

A lot of people say where only having the one parent is bad, but I never got on with Alice, that's our mother. She got knocked down and killed when I was twelve but I never missed her much. She was one of these really bossy people, really thought she was king of the castle.

When Eric and me was little, guess what Bike Man used to make us do? Bike Man had us learning all the specs of every bike he had by heart, right? Two little kids chanting away like they was learning their nursery rhymes or them old-fashioned times tables Alice used to moan about them not teaching us no more. I can still remember them specs, some of them. Listen, this is Bike Man's A65L Lightning. *ENGINE : BSA six hundred and fifty-four cubic centimetre overhead valve parallel twin crankshaft supported in plain and roller bearings* and me and Eric'd be chanting away there because Bike Man used to make us say them faster and faster and time us with a stop-watch to beat the world record *plain big-end bearings light alloy cylinder-head compression ratio nine to one dry-sump lubrication oil-tank capacity five and a half pints CARBURETTORS : two Amal Monoblocs with air filters air slides operated by handlebar levers* and we used to get really good at it because I was always good at learning things by heart even when I didn't understand it and so was Eric, only I think Eric understood some of them specs *ELECTRICAL EQUIPMENT : Lucas twin-coil twin contact-breaker ignition with auto-advance Lucas twelve-volt RM 19 alternator with rotor on drive-side crankshaft charging twin Lucas six-volt thirteen amp-hour batteries through rectifier Zener diode regulator* and Bike Man'd be waving us on quicker and quicker like he was Sir Otto Bonkers conducting the runaway train with his stopwatch *TRANSMISSION : BSA four-speed foot-change gearbox with engine ratios bottom twelve point oh three six second seven point six seven third five point four eight top four point eight seven to one multi-plate clutch with bonded friction-facing primary chain three-eighths triplex in oil-bath case* and Eric and me'd be bouncing up and down to try and make ourselves go faster only we couldn't gabble nothing because Bike Man said no gabbling and if we did we had to start again and we always got so we could say the last bit really fast with no gabbling *BSA Motorcycles Limited Armoury Road Small Heath Birmingham-Eleven!* And Bike Man'd look at his watch and jump in the air and shout, 'It's a record! It's a record!' and me and Eric'd cheer and clap and Martin would give us 50p and Alice would look at him like he was gone nutty only she couldn't stop completely smiling at the same time, right?

Alice was a real snob, you know? It was like she couldn't forgive her husband and kids for not being famous enough to impress her friends with. Eric used to say to wear your steel toecaps to Alice's party due to where she dropped names hard enough to break your foot. Before Eric was born, Alice used to be an actress on the stage. Plus she was once the Nimble lady in the telly commercial, only that was before I was born and I never seen it because they don't do repeats of old commercials like they do with the films. She was really strange about it anyway, Alice, like when she talked about it she was all at once showing off about being famous and at the same time as if it was something to almost be ashamed of. Anyway, I couldn't do that, not go on the stage with all them people. I mean, they'd all *see* you, wouldn't they? And I really don't miss Alice at all, hardly. I don't even mind where Martin is going on and on about her the whole time, because that's his problem, right?

Eric misses her. If Eric ever does do Martin, it'll be because Martin will not leave off going on and on about Alice.

Sometimes I think Martin ain't really Bike Man at all no more. Bike Man would be Sean and Wayne's friend and not only grunt at them plus sneer at their bike. He would take me and Eric for illegal burns round the South Circular with Eric on the pillion and me on the tank, which is the illegal bit, also no crash helmet although maybe that wasn't illegal yet then. Only he couldn't do that now due to where we're too big, and especially Eric. All right, maybe Wayne and Sean and them do look a bit heavy with all the biker gear and studs and crossbones and tattoos and that, but I mean I remember some of the bike geezers Bike Man used to bring home when he was little and they used to look like fucking Godzilla. Plus Eric always said Martin himself was the original model for the Ogri strip in *Bike*. (Did you see where they dropped that strip? One they got now's really poncey.) Plus a smart geezer like Martin's got to be able to suss out what me and Eric can see plain as anything, which is that Wayne and Sean and the rest only come on heavy because they think if they don't people will take them for a wimp and someone will pick on them.

Anyway, I think Wayne and Sean look really tasty, and especially Wayne. Wayne is nineteen, which is a year older than Eric and that makes Wayne feel bad about being scared of him. I wouldn't feel bad about being scared of Eric if I was a boy due to any boy not scared of Eric needs his brains tested. When Eric was fifteen and Alice was still alive and Martin was still Bike Man a lot of the time and Eric still used to help him with the bikes, Martin used to call him the Human Hoist because he was strong enough to carry about bits of Squariel in his hands that by rights they should have had a hoist for. But Wayne really do feel bad about being scared of him. Wayne don't *say* nothing about feeling bad; he don't even say nothing about being scared, right? He wouldn't, would he? But I *know* all right. I got this sensitivity for the way Wayne feels without him saying nothing. Sometimes I think me and Wayne was made for each other because we don't really need to speak to know the way the other one feels. Which is just as well because Wayne don't speak much at the best of times. Sean says Wayne could be the strong silent type if he was strong, but Wayne says, 'You want to find out how strong, you know where to reach me,' and Sean always makes a joke out of it. When Wayne does talk, it's nearly always heavy stuff like that he says. He ain't no use at making people laugh, not like Sean, so he thinks the only way he can make you like him and have respect is to come across heavy like the Maniac Biker from Hell, and he thinks nobody will see it's really only Wayne Simpson from Lewisham underneath. And maybe old people like Martin don't, maybe it's like the way they all get to need glasses, right?

Wayne and Sean are both of them despatch riders for this radio-control express delivery company. Sean is quite happy at it but he thinks the whole of life is one big laugh and I bet Sean would be happy at any job where he gets to ride bikes. Wayne hates it, though. All Wayne wants to be all day is King Horror Death on Wheels, all stubble and leather and Eat my

Dust and two-mile wheelies with the jam sandwiches running
for their life and the dwarf-brain old wimp pedestrians and
motorists struck dumb with terror and the kids all cheering
every time Our Hero roars past and especially the girls and
especially *me*. And instead he has to take all this shit over the
radio from some pot-bellied old fart in a back-alley office in
Deptford about pick up envelope from J. Bogrich Solicitors in
Eltham High Street and when you done that pick up a Red
Star from South Croydon Station and generally be at the beck
and call of old uncle Tom Cobblers and all and it never lets
up, right? But Wayne says what else can you do because you
can't run even a GPz550H2 on fresh air plus what he really
fancies is a Pantah if not a Mike Hailwood Replica. And he
says if I got my sights set on a mortgaged semi in Grove Park
with designer video trolley to fucking forget it, girl, because
with him the Bike must Come First and be his Main Thing.

Eric don't like bikers but he says where he has a lot of
sympathy for Wayne, because he ain't never going to do no
shit job for nobody. He says why should a free man shovel
shit if he don't need the money but Martin chips in with if he
needs the money he ain't free and Eric tells him to bog off,
smartarse. Martin says stuff like that all the time because he's
a socialist At Heart only he is the richest socialist At Heart in
Blackheath Village and Eric says where that's saying something, right? Martin is in Advertising and people pay him
thousands of pounds to do ads about lager and hi-fi and
building societies so they will all buy it.

He never sent us to no private schools like him and Alice
was at due to that would be a class thing and make the
comprehensive schools not work by keeping out the rich kids
who would be a Good Influence. And then when we end up
talking like the other kids due to if you talk posh they laugh at
you or worse, and when we come down here to drink instead
of the poncey Albion where we only ever went because you
can sit in the garden and send in someone who looks over age

17

to get the drinks, Martin goes on and on and *on* about it, right? Do that stand up when you think about it? Do it?

As well as going on about Alice and the way me and Eric look and behave and that, Martin is also always on at us about politics and the Future of our Society and What are we going to make of our Life, right? Him and Eric have these bleeding great arguments about politics and stuff whenever Eric ain't in a Bollocks mood. I don't join in these politics arguments due to half the time I don't get what they're driving at, but I'll tell you one thing. I don't know who this wally is who gives us all these politics lectures, but it sure as shit ain't Bike Man, right?

It's really good here, not like the poncey Albion where you practically got to have a visa from the British Ambassador to prove you're old enough to have a drink. Also Martin is always liable to turn up pissed and show you up rotten. And twice a week it gets even worse because the poxy Runners come in. There's about a hundred and one of them and they all go running round the Heath for miles and miles and then they all come in the Albion at once in their sweaty trainers and track-suits and stuff, right? And you can't bleeding move in the bar for them and they all shout at the top of their voice about where they come in the East Dogturd half-marathon and their weekly mileage and their boring fucking shin-splints, and they push and pose and yell in the regulars' ear trying to get the bar staff attention for one lager shandy and sixteen pints of soda water *with ice*, and they do Athlete faces and show each other photos of themself running and search for their own name in running mags to show everybody. Plus they smell like Sock Death Poo. And this is grown-ups, right, including old farts even older than Martin? Mostly I think Wayne will some day grow out of the worst bits of his Thundershit Highway Outlaw pose, but when I see them Runners, it makes you think. To me, I think if I was like them I'd run like shit to get as far away from myself as soon as

possible, right? I don't go in the Albion no more, and especially
not on Runners nights.

They got really good music here, too. Not now, but later on.
And they don't put the price of the drink up double when the
band starts like some places. I used to think the reason Eric
don't like bikers is the music, due to Sean and Wayne and the
rest all hate everything except heavy metal dead loud. Eric
says the sort of stuff they like is just noise and pain and you
can't call it music unless you got brain damage plus your deaf
aid switched off or else no ears.

When we was younger and Bike Man used to drive us all
down to Santa Pod in the Range Rover, Eric always used to
bags-I the cassette player and play all Martin's old Floyd and
String Band and Joni Mitchell tapes all the way and if Alice
was with us she would ask him whether we *have* to, Eric?
But Bike Man would stand up for Eric against her over the
music, which is funny because he never done it over anything
else, right? And Alice would just have to sit there and listen
to it all the way with her Oh God face on, only Alice didn't
hardly ever come with us anyway.

Now when Eric goes in the loft to pump iron he plays all
Alice's old records of organ music by Bach and such loud
enough to shake the floor and Mrs Koenig next door rings up
to complain, only if Eric answers it he tells her to bog off or he
will come round there and bite the goolies off her wolfhound
plus rape the goat and Mrs Koenig stops ringing for a week or
two. Eric is very touchy about having his concentration broke
when he is pumping iron, right? He says where you could do
yourself a mischief. To me, anyone worried about that will
have more sense than lie on their back and hump bleeding
great chunks of metal twice as heavy as theirself up and down
in their sweaty hand. I don't really like to watch Eric pump
iron. His face goes asleep and his eyes look wrong like his
brain was gone out to lunch and it makes me come over
funny.

19

The way people fight about the music is really stupid. I mean, it's not just the kids ganging up into Jazz Funkers kill Rockawally Shit and Northern Soul Posse run Punk Junk which is just using it for an excuse, like a coachload of Charlton Athletic skins stopped at the lights giving the Wanker sign to all the people going past ain't really into football, right? But it's the grown-ups too with the music, ain't it?

I mean, Martin would come in the house with Alice playing Radio Three through his Quad which nobody but Martin is supposed to touch and he would put on his Bike-Man-Him-Heap-Mad-Run-for-the-Hills face only this time Him *really* Heap Mad not just an act to frighten me when we was little. And he wouldn't say a thing and leave the radio alone and quietly put one of his own albums on the deck and wait till it gets to a loud bit only it's still the radio coming through, right? Then he flips the switch from Tuner to Aux and whacks the volume up at the same time so we go straight from the Heavenly Choirboys of Oxford College to a two-hour drum solo by Ginger Bonkers which will burst your eardrums next door, right? And Alice would come rushing through from the kitchen and her face would be a real picture, because she is very into Rules and doing Right and she knows she have broke a Rule by playing Martin's Quad, but at the same time Alice is *very* heavily into Winning and pissed off this time because she can't win *and* be Right. But when it comes to Winning v. being Right it is no fucking contest where Alice is concerned and she pulls the plug at the mains and Martin and her have this really terrific fight. About the music, right? Any other fight they have, Alice may as well not bother because she will be talking to herself. Martin will let her rant and rave until he thinks she have got it Out of her System plus duck when she throws stuff, and then he makes a little quiet pause. And then he says, 'Well, yes and no.'

Eric says this is their secret password for having a flag of truce and mostly it works. But when it comes to the music, Bike Man Strikes Back. He says where she is brainwashed by her snob education due to people telling her it is Great Art when she is little and she says how he is shallow and has no Soul and is a deliberate philistine on purpose and pretty soon they are just shouting and it don't really matter the words they use. And in the finish Bike Man always says to sod it and stomps off down to the Albion or roars off into the Night on Bike of the Month due to Bike Man is more into Peace and Quiet and Fun and Games than he is into Winning. And Alice is left listening to the Heavenly Choirboys but still not sure she has really Won. Eric says Bike Man never loses a music fight; he just makes a tactical withdrawal. Eric used to tell me stuff where he reads that people in history always been fighting over music, like where everybody's Mum and Dad always think their kids' music is rubbish, if not a Sin, and Eric thinks maybe the kids always choose their music like that to keep it to theirself. Also really poncey old fart concert audiences going nutty and smashing the place up over some avant-garde stuff that ten years later they all say is a Wonderful Masterpiece. To me, I think you either like a music or you don't. Plus the real reason Eric don't like bikers ain't nothing to do with music anyway.

Even when we was quite little kids, Eric was very into reading books. Like he would always have a book as well when Alice plonks us in front of 'Jackanory' so she can go off and drink vodka in the kitchen with Jenny Prendergast and talk about the Stage and who is knocking off who and the Price of Everything, my dear. And mostly Eric *reads* his book too, and makes me go and listen at the door so he can know what they are saying and not spoil his book, right? He is even worse now. When Eric reads a book, the whole world could disappear around him, *whomp*, and he would not even see it. To me, I just can't see what he gets out of it. I mean, some books got useful stuff in such as cookbooks and How to

Adjust your Rear Chain and the capital of Sri Lanka, but what Eric reads is just *stories*. Why would you want to spend your time reading a story that someone only made up out of their head? Not me.

It is beyond me why Eric do miss Alice, right? She would treat him just as shitty as me and never give him no peace to do what he wants, which is all Eric was ever really after. She would say to him about why don't he have no friends his own age and mooning around the house the whole time instead of go out in the fresh air plus he should play sport and be in a Team because it will do him Good and he will be grateful to her for it in Later Life just like practising the piano and stuff like that all the time. I used to feel really sorry for him only thankful at the same time I wasn't the one getting it for once, right? Any fool can see that Eric do not have any friends because he do not want any, and a good thing too because the other kids are all too shit scared of Eric to be his friend. Which is a laugh really, because Eric will not hurt a fly provided they leave him alone. Eric do not have it in him to bite the goolies off nobody's wolfhound, which is just a pose to get old Bogface Koenig out of his ear. But the other kids are so scared of him that they don't take the piss out of him over *nothing*, not even good exam marks or playing a Beethoven sonata in the concert. Not even Sean and Wayne and Ferret Dave and Michael Christopoulos and all those other nutters in the year above him. Alice really makes me puke when I think about her going on and on and *on* to Eric to bring his friends round the house because if Eric *did* bring home someone like Wayne or Ferret Dave Alice would not touch them with a bargepole and in fact she would not even touch the bargepole. Plus have a go at Martin afterwards about his stupid ideas on comprehensive education and I do not think Alice is a socialist even At Heart. And if she was still alive when *I* brung Sean and Wayne home she would have a kitten plus do her pieces and make Martin and Eric look like Mister

Welcome. But Eric do miss her, even if he don't say nothing about it, right? Do that stand up when you think about it? Do it?

When Wayne takes me on his pillion and we go out on the motorway and find some nice bendy country roads to scratch along, it is really good. Especially if we are by ourself, not with Sean and Ferret Dave and Bastard Jack and whole gang of other bikers. If we are by ourself, it is nearly as good as when we used to go with Bike Man. Maybe it *is* as good, because Eric says you always remember a thing better than it really is at the time. I think I see what Eric is driving at, but also I think it really was even better with Bike Man. Alice would try to stop us going for a burn, surprise surprise; she says because it's too dangerous but we always know she just cannot stand to see anyone have fun she can't join in herself. But Bike Man knows how much me and Eric like it so he takes us anyway, though he will usually pick us up and drop us off at the corner or somewhere unless he has already had a music fight with Alice, in which case there is Nothing to Lose, men. And off we go on the Trident or the Commando or the Bonneville or the Thruxton, sometimes all three of us but mostly just Bike Man and Eric or just Bike Man and me. Bike Man does not do any heavy Highway Nightmare shit but he is funny and brave and clever and when me and Eric are out with him we want it to always be like this. He makes us swear joke oaths of secrecy and Death to the Fug-box Punter, and he wears an old RAF greatcoat with big badges on it saying WHO BE DO BE DO FRANK SINATRA? and GOD SET FIRE TO THE DUKE OF IRELAND and stuff like that which he gets done special at the office. And on the Daytona he fiddled the wiring so he could switch the stop-light on and off without touching the brake and take the piss out of any poxy car driver who gets up his nose, and he lets us work the switch for a treat and it is called Going Through the Motions of Stopping. And Little Do We Think that one day Bike Man will

23

be No More and we will be left with only this prize nerd Martin with a non-runner Squariel in his garage plus a Porsche 911T with a sticker on the back saying MY OTHER CAR IS A PORSCHE only he can't drive it due to he got breathalysed. We should have seen it coming when Bike of the Month started getting older and older and *older*. I mean, the one before the Squariel was a Gold Star from bleeding 1950 or something, though at least it was a runner. Sean says where the Squariel will never run no more due to Martin would have sorted it years before now if he really wanted to. Plus he says nobody with any sense will give it houseroom except in an antique shop and even if Martin do want it to run again he will be hard pushed to make it into a decent motor-mower.

The real reason Eric don't like bikers is this. It is a biker that run Alice down and killed her. I didn't know nothing about this for *years* afterwards, right? Nobody tells me a bleeding thing about it. Martin and Eric both know about it because they were there but you can't even speak to Martin about it for years afterwards and you *still* can't speak to Eric about it. Not even Martin can speak to Eric about it and Live to Tell the Tale. But Martin will tell me about it nowadays if he is pissed up and Eric ain't about, and in fact he has told me about it so often I always feel like next time when he starts I will tell him to fucking leave it out just like Eric do. But I never bring myself to do it due to he does this Tragedy face and acts very Be Brave Little Girl and looks so bleeding *pathetic* that you do not have the heart. I look at him and his red eyes shining and his sweaty fat face and his bald hair and his voice all trembly and you can't really be shitty to him no more than you can kick a lame dog, but at the same time you can't help thinking that This Man is the Ultimate Wally. When he is not in a Bog Off mood, Eric sometimes says to me to not think too badly of Martin due to where he is really Defeated by Life, but to me it is No fucking Contest. He always makes a great Drama speech out of it and you would

24

bet he rehearses it in the bog or something only he is always so pissed up when he tells me that no way can he remember anything he have learnt by heart.

They are down the shopping centre that Bike Man calls the Really Pedestrian Precinct plus they got a really high office tower with the brown mirror windows. And Alice always goes on about how ugly it looks with no Soul and it makes the whole place not human due to it is on a too big scale plus it always channels the wind down into a bleeding gale, except Alice don't ever say 'bleeding'. And Eric always says, 'Yes. Just like a Cathedral.' So Eric and Alice are never on very good terms in the Really Pedestrian Precinct, even though Eric is not grown into his Rat Off stage then. But it is the light and the way it makes the reflection in this mirror block look that Martin always starts off about when he tells me. He says where it proves that if there is someone Up There, they must be taking the piss to shine a beautiful light like that on something so really terrible. He never tells me the details of the fight Eric and Alice have and I don't know if this is because he has forgot it or because he never noticed at the time, but I bet Bike Man never noticed. To me, I bet it was all Alice's fault going on and on at Eric about whatever it was because that is what she always does and maybe Eric even before he is Bog Off Man do sometimes pass smartarse remarks but he never starts a fight with Alice or even lips her back. And I bet Eric runs away because Alice goes Too Far and Eric knows if he do not run away he can't stop himself giving her a right-hander and he knows how shitty he will feel if he do. To me, this is just what Eric would do. All Martin says about it is where he couldn't do nothing to stop it, could he, due to it happens so quick and God God Mandy you know what she is Like when she Starts, right? Plus nobody makes Alice chase after Eric who is quite old enough to look after himself and I think she only does it because she has to be sure she Wins and I bet Eric do not even know she is behind him when he skips across the road plus she has to be nutty or something or at least need her eyes tested to run straight out without looking and *whomp*.

Martin always says he is sorry for the poor biker who has no chance. The biker is dead too, right? The poor sod goes straight under a truck. Plus he is quite an old geezer. So it really do not stand up when you think about it that Eric don't like bikers, do it? And anyway, this was bleeding *years* ago and I do not think it is healthy for Eric to still miss Alice and *I* don't miss her at all, right?

In the middle of it all with the ambulances and everything, Bike Man can't stop himself noticing that the dead bike is a mint 1938 Speed Twin. And he is so mixed up he goes and tells Eric and after that Eric will not say a single word to him for a whole year and more, not even 'Bollocks', and I do not think Martin is ever completely Bike Man again and even now Eric mostly don't say nothing only 'Bollocks' and 'Sod off.'

And another thing that don't stand up. You will say it is only natural for a girl to like her dad, but what about when you think of a total nerd like Martin? It do not stand up when you think about it that anyone would like a total nerd like Martin whether or not he is her dad, do it?

So why do I *like* Martin?

Right?

A SMALL DIFFERENCE ONLY

For Clive Blenkinsop

Such a small difference can change the whole truth and nothing but the truth into a lie totally, my friend. Such a small difference in the words one is using or in the tone of the voice or in the expression of the face or even in the hearts and minds of the listeners only. Look around you and listen in truly alert fashion and I tell you that you will hear for yourself what I mean. Every day my working circumstances in the shop ensure that I am listening to people talk amongst the bosom of their family and friends and I am telling you that it is a most unusual day when I do not hear at least one truly horrendous misunderstanding of this kind, where the message transmitted, *over*, bears no correspondence whatsoever to the message received, *roger and out*. And we speak here for the most part of native-born mother-tongue speakers of the Queen's English. Think, then, of how it must be for persons such as my good self for whom the Queen's English comes truly as a foreign language. Think of the truly horrendous potential for misunderstanding of this nature in both directions.

Sometimes the effect is amusing only. I well remember when I was first able to bring over the good lady wife from her family home in Uttar Pradesh. My friend, before she is across the threshold she is issuing instructions already. 'Patel,' she is saying, 'you must paint the front of the shop directly. The paintwork is dingy dingy. If I am a passing customer, I will surely think that any businessman who keeps his premises in such condition is truly lackadaisical. I will worry that he keeps goods of similar ilk to his premises and I will shop elsewhere.' I translate, of course. At this date, the good

Mrs P is speaking no English whatsoever. She is speaking it very little even now, when she understands it very well indeed. She is quite correct about the condition of the paintwork, but even if this were not the case, I think I would still be doing the painting. The good Mrs P is a jewel beyond price but she has always had a mind of her own and I am a peaceful man. I am very quickly learning that the good Mrs P becomes most unhappy when crossed in matters domestic and is a true adept at sharing her unhappiness. I believe most sincerely that it is truly foolish to court unhappiness, my friend. To cut a long story short, yours truly is soon to be seen with paint-brush in hand rendering the exterior of the premises a most cheerful shade of royal blue. 'Patel,' the good Mrs P is saying, 'if a customer or even a passer-by only is damaging his clothing on your wet paint, it will be truly bad for business and may even involve litigation. You must erect a warning notice directly.' And so I am writing out just such a notice in large capital letters on a convenient piece of cardboard cut by yours truly from an old Bird's Custard carton and affixing same to shop window with Sellotape, then returning to the matter of the royal blue. Better to be safe than to be sorry, after all is said and done. But shortly thereafter it is beginning to become apparent to me that all is not quite as it should be. I am uncomfortably aware of something amiss in the comportment of persons passing close by. They are staring more severely than one would be expecting and in cases where they are in groups I am detecting signs of amusement or perhaps contempt. I am beginning to wonder whether the choice of royal blue is truly a happy one. I am even at one point surreptitiously checking to see whether I require, excuse me, an adjustment to the trousers, but all is well in that particular department.

But then it is occurring to me to examine instead the warning notice, and all is instantly clear. One letter only, such a small difference, but the message is transformed utterly.

The warning notice inadvertently is reading: WET PANT.

Many years before this particular event, when I am first coming to these shores as a young man to seek my fame and my fortune, I am making a surprising and unpleasant discovery. As I sally forth to amass myself a comfortable nest-egg which will enable me to become an independent businessman in my own right, I am truly astonished to discover that I am not speaking English. All my life until then I am thinking quite happily that yours truly is a fluent speaker of the Queen's English and indeed the King's English at an earlier date. At home in Uttar Pradesh we are sometimes speaking practically nothing else for days on end, since practically everyone who has anything to do with the Patel household is speaking and understanding at least some of said noble tongue, my friend. But in a few days only after my disembarkation, I am made to realize that what I am speaking so fluently fluently is a fine language in its own right, no doubt, but it is not the Queen's English. Not quite. Yours truly is very often finding extreme difficulty in making himself understood by the good citizens of old London town. Two, three, four times and more I am repeating myself when I am asking directions or purchasing supplies in a shop and sometimes even then I am still not understood. My fine career ambitions are having to take a nasty jolt, my friend, and I would say very largely owing to this business of the Queen's English. With my fine BA (Honours) degree apparently set at nought by the various employers of old London town and added to this the business of the Queen's English, yours truly is successful in finding employment as lowly Clerical Assistant only in the General Post Office Telephones. At the time I am greatly afraid that the family will find out about my predicament and blame me for it. I am writing to tell them I am Civil Servant, which is no more than the truth but somewhat less than the whole truth and nothing but the truth. I do not dare to tell them I am on the very bottom rung only of the Civil

Service grading ladder and that my duties consist of licking sticky labels and fetching and filing papers and ordering fresh supplies of pens, blotters, elastic bands and other stationery sundries and brewing tea. How can I possibly tell the parents who have all my life skimped and saved to educate their son to the highest university level and send him to England to find his fame and his fortune that I am become dogsbody only?

What is baffling me so much at first is that the Queen's English and the language I am speaking so fluently are so very nearly the same. I am forming the theory that I must study very closely the difference between what yours truly is speaking and the Queen's English, because even though this difference is so small, small it is enough to assure yours truly a lifetime career as Clerical Assistant if I am not eliminating said difference. A Clerical Assistant who is sending home sufficient of his weekly wages to impress suitably his aged parents is most unlikely to amass any sort of nest-egg, my friend. So I am beginning to think all the time about exactly what my English colleagues are saying and writing at the office. It makes me smile when I think about it nowadays, my friend, but the young man who is an earlier edition of yours truly is taking it very seriously indeed. And with completely straight face he is listening to Major Lennox, who is wartime promotion only to Major in the Territorials and is in peacetime guise risen to dizzy heights of Higher Clerical Officer only, read his *Daily Express* each lunchtime and regularly say to himself, 'Good grief!' And the so serious young man is thinking, *What could be good about it*? Or three times a week he will hear Miss Lynch make yet again her solitary joke at his expense, 'Ah, but Mr Patel is a horse of a different colour.' *But I am not a horse*, the so serious young man is thinking. 'How is the cold, Patel?' Major Lennox is saying, 'Been to the doctor with it?' *How can I be going to the doctor without it*? the so earnest young Mr Patel is asking himself. And the so serious young Mr Patel is realizing that his life is not long enough for him to solve his problem simply by close observations of how the Queen's English is used by the Queen's English and by constant meditations upon same. He is realizing there are nearly as many versions of the Queen's English as there are speakers of it, and that constant meditations upon even one version only will very likely drive a saint to delinquency. And he is forming new theory that one cannot learn how to speak a language by constant meditations. It must be done by practice, as is the case with learning to ride a bicycle. Constant meditations upon the detailed mechanics of riding bicycles while actually engaged upon doing same will have inevitable consequences, he is realizing. One falls off.

So yours truly in his younger guise is ceasing to brood about the subtleties of his adoptive native tongue and waiting patiently for his everyday practice of listening to same and speaking and reading it in due course to render him truly an expert or at any rate a passably competent user of it. And though he is a quiet and self-effacing young man, he has no real doubt he will succeed in his noble enterprise. He has the confidence all young persons have when they are still truly believing themselves to be living forever with all things possible in the best of all possible worlds. And indeed life seems to be reluctant to discourage this so earnest young person's optimism, my friend. After a few months only, he is growing almost bold.

At this time, the more juvenile edition of yours truly is in the habit of patronizing the excellent staff canteen at India House in the Aldwych. The world is a different place in those days, my friend, and one can walk into most embassies and the like and be quite unchallenged by armed officers of the law and other manifestations of security arrangements. Such things are still many years into the so serious young man's future. And the staff canteen at India House is not advertised by so much as a small exterior notice, yet still it is being patronized by nearly as many Asian members of the general public as by the actual staff of the establishment. The food is excellent and besides which it is cheap cheap. It is one quarter the price only of the Indian restaurants patronized by mother-tongue speakers of the Queen's English. But at one point it appears to our young man that things culinary at this eating place are taking a decided turn for the worse. Perhaps a new *chef de cuisine* is being employed, he cannot say, but he is noticing that all his favourite spicy dishes are now becoming not spicy only but truly hot hot to the point of being extremely uncomfortable to eat. He is in somewhat of a quandary. As an outsider using the facilities on sufferance only, he feels doubtful of having rights of personal complaint to management personnel of said facilities, besides being of a retiring disposition. And he has also heard more than one of his fellow patrons remark favourably upon the new gustatory developments and fears himself to be in small minority only. But then the great idea is striking him. He will place a notice of modest protest upon staff notice-board of said canteen. Said notice must be in English, since by regular observation he is determining that this appears to be the invariable protocol for notices upon said notice-board. This necessity of composition in the Queen's English gives rise to no little misgivings on the part of our so earnest young man. By now, he is becoming truly confident about his expertise in listening to and reading and even speaking the Queen's English, but in writing it he has scant practice only. But if nothing is ventured, nothing is gained, after all is said and done. Three whole lunch-hours he is devoting to the mental composition of his notice whilst strolling around the streets in lieu of consuming the lately-lethal vindaloo. On the fourth day, his immediate superior Miss Lynch is surprising him at his desk red-handed in the very act of committing his message in large block capitals to the surface of a postcard, and he is feeling obliged to explain to her the nature of his enterprise. Indeed he is at least partly pleased to have been detected, since he is feeling that perhaps knowledge of this escapade will engender in colleagues and superiors alike new-found respect for him as man of principle and action, not to mention competent executant of notices in the Queen's English. Please not to think too badly of this so serious long-ago young man, my friend. Yours truly has learnt in time to think of him without embarrassment or contempt. 'Mr Patel has written a notice,' Miss Lynch is announcing to her superior in turn, namely the said Major Lennox, 'Mr Patel is going to make a gesture of protest.' Major Lennox is making his formerly so baffling remark upon the goodness of grief and examining said postcard, and then repeating his remark, and then passing the postcard to everyone in turn in the whole office with the requisite oral explanations. There is much nodding of heads and raising of eyebrows and glancing in the direction of the young man, who is smiling shyly and truly basking in the unwonted attention, my friend. But as his postcard is returned to him and he is making his departure, an awful truth is dawning upon him. Despite being no great natural student of languages, our young man is not imperceptive altogether, and he sees that the so polite Queen's English faces of his colleagues and superiors are not quite successful in concealing true feelings of amusement and, yes, pity. So the young man is hurrying away with his postcard but he is never affixing it to the said notice-board for fear of rendering himself an object of mockery and derision. I have said postcard to this day, my friend, and our so earnest young man is making correct decision.

Said postcard reads in barely legible penmanship: MORE CHILLIES DOES NOT MAKE GOOD TASTES BUT BURN THE INTESTINES ONLY.

As time goes by our solemn young friend is realizing that he is never going to become a truly expert speaker of the Queen's English and certainly never an expert writer of it.

His speaking and listening attainments improve to a degree where he is competent indeed on a day-to-day business and social level, but no blind person is ever going to mistake him for mother-tongue speaker of the Queen's English by any manner or means. Our young friend is able to obtain employment in various part-time capacities provided always he is willing to undertake low-status tasks about which he may by no means write to his aged parents, but this is of scant concern to him. By holding several such jobs concurrently and working long long hours, our young man can at long last start to amass his nest-egg. Our hero is admitting to himself he is not in danger of becoming the social toast of old London town or even of old Goldhawk Road only, but he is thinking that he is en route for a rewarding and maybe even noteworthy commercial career. He is willing to perform low-status tasks shunned by mother-tongue speakers of the nation's lingua franca because he is a philosophical young man. He reasons that to do degrading tasks without feelings of degradation is sign of inner strength, not of weakness as believed by those who shun such tasks.

Time passes.

A nest-egg is amassed.

The proprietorship of a commercial enterprise is purchased.

A marriage is arranged.

A lot is to be said, my friend, for a quiet and orderly existence and the eschewment of overweening ambition entirely. In childhood, yours truly and siblings are frequently regaled by parents and grandparents with the awful example of Great-Uncle Inventor Patel, an inhabitant of the preceding century anno domini. This esteemed relative is seemingly a natural mechanical genius, we are told. We are further told that he is a person of overweening ambition. Crowning achievement of Inventor Patel's career is elevator safety brake, patent pending. This predates, we are told, subsequent inventions in the same field by Occidental engineers such as

Westinghouse and Otis. Principle of Inventor Patel's safety brake is similar to these later inventions, however. Sudden slackening of tension on attachment to supporting cable of lift, such as will occur at times of cable failure, operates catch mechanism which frees a system of sturdy steel rods stowed beneath and parallel to floor of passenger compartment under powerful spring pressure. Release of said catch under emergency conditions allows said rods to be projected vigorously out of the walls of the lift compartment, striking the inner walls of the shaft still under spring pressure and holding said compartment safely in place by friction until the requisite assistance is arriving.

The day of the public demonstration of the great invention is coming. Lift in question is installed in new grand hotel building in Delhi and progressive management of same are desirous of displaying to their potential clientele amongst the moneyed classes their zeal and concern for the safety of their esteemed lives and limbs. Great-Uncle Inventor is somewhat of an exhibitionist, we are told. He is showing his faith in his own invention and at the same time exposing himself to the maximum possible attention and acclaim. He is positioning himself alone within the lift compartment which is then suspended between the third and fourth floor levels. The suspension cable is then deliberately cut, with due ceremonial as befits such an auspicious occasion. Alas, Inventor P has sadly miscalculated. The force of his springs and the weight of his steel rods is such that they are not striking the inner walls of the lift shaft only, my friend, they are demolishing said walls. Furthermore, two of said walls are of load-bearing nature, and extensive collapse of fifth and higher floors structure in immediate vicinity of said shaft ensues forthwith with truly horrendous consequences. The lifeless remains of Inventor Patel are coming to rest at the very bottom of said shaft forcibly mingled with the broken remnants of said lift compartment and buried beneath many many tons of assorted masonry and woodwork and dead and injured citizens. And all, we are told, because of overweening ambition and showing off.

Actually, my friend, our chief infant reaction to the tale of Great-Uncle Inventor is one of amusement, but it is very plain to us from the manner in which it is told that the tale is not one at which one is permitted to laugh or even to smile only. Nowadays I am thinking moral of story is really lethal danger of excessive zeal for safety. But despite juvenile amusement, I somehow think the sorry fate of poor Inventor P is making deep unconscious impression upon yours truly, for all my adult days it has been my invariable personal inclination to eschew the pursuit of fame and ostentation and to settle for modest security.

But there is always the question of the good lady wife. This jewel amongst women is as exquisitely unobtrusive and deferential in the public gaze as any husband could desire, even from the very outset of our marriage. The good Mrs P is the product of a very thorough upbringing, my friend. Many times over the years male customers are remarking on this noteworthy fact and complimenting me upon same. 'What is the secret of your success, my old mate?' they are asking me. 'How do you do it?' I am smiling only and saying nothing, for who will be trusting walls to remain deaf? In the privacy of our own domestic circles, matters are quite differently arranged. It is, 'Patel, you must take up with the representative of the gum-vending machine the question of the old half-pennies. It is his company's fault their so stupid machine believes them to be two new pence instead of one-tenth that value only. An allowance should be made. We are losing money.' We are losing on average precisely 12 new pence per week, my friend, on turnover in excess of £4 per machine and retail mark-up of 20 per centum. And Mr Gupta the Gudi-Gudi agent is inoffensive and aging individual much troubled by sciatica and the paucity of his commission as compared with the ambitions of his own good lady wife. 'Patel,' Mrs P is saying, 'you must get a motor van directly. We will be increasing business if you are offering delivery service and also it is most belittling to me to be last mother remaining in Jasbir's school class who is escorting child to school on foot only. Van will be more practical than car, also more cheap.' If only the good Mrs P's upbringing and education would permit her to be putting such arguments so forcefully and repeatedly to yours truly's bank manager, my friend! 'Patel,' she is saying, 'look here in this magazine, where is article relating how penniless Parsee immigrant in ten years only is becoming multi-millionaire businessman and owning luxury mansion house in Brent Green with marble floor ballroom and indoor swimming-pool!' *In English climate*, I am thinking, *outdoor swimming-pool will be in great danger of getting wet in the rain*, but I am not by any manner or means communicating this thought to Mrs P. The good Mrs P is a jewel beyond price, my friend, but it is unfortunate fact that she is invariably interpreting humorous remarks as personal insults.

In early years of our so-long marriage, pressures such as the immediately aforesaid from the good Mrs P are quite unrelenting. They are causing yours truly to worry worry the whole day long and large stretches of the night watches also. Two-feet length of the old intestine is having to be removed surgically to combat resulting ulcer, my friend, and perhaps it is this incident which is causing the good lady wife to become at long last less strident in her demands for the advancement of our fame and our fortune. Not silent, by any manner or means, but decidedly less strident. And myself, I am getting unexpected bonus when doctor's orders for unstressful and orderly existence are aligning exactly with yours truly's true personal inclinations. Dr Heinrich Fischer, who is not medical doctor but who is a lifelong customer of the Patel family business and forever ready to offer words of jovial advice and wisdom, is a hearty supporter of said regimen.

'Ach, my dear Patel, it is just so we order our affairs in my homeland.' Dr Heinrich Fischer is Swiss gentleman. 'We are accustomed to orderly and temperate behaviour in all things. In the United States, Patel, they sell guns to all and sundry who have not been instructed in orderly and temperate behaviour, and you may every day read how someone has run amok and shoots down his fellow citizens in the street. Yet in my homeland, every male adult is compelled by law to keep a rifle and ammunition in his home as part of our national defence arrangements, but none runs ever amok. We have our share of mental disturbance as does every country, but we are instructed in orderly and temperate behaviour. Our orderly and temperate disturbed Swiss male runs never amok with his government rifle, for he has been made to *sign for the bullets*, Patel.' The good Mrs P, I am thankful to say, is setting great store by the wisdom of Dr Heinrich Fischer, and the more so because he is professional gentleman who is never submitting bill for said wisdom.

But if the good lady wife is becoming resigned over the years to the necessity of an orderly and temperate existence for yours truly, this does not mean that her own overweening ambition is becoming a thing of the past only. Not by any manner or means, my friend. The good Mrs P quite unaided generates overweening ambition in such truly horrendous quantities that she must find an outlet for it or she will burst directly. Fortunately for all concerned, my friend, the ideal outlet is conveniently to hand. It is our son Jasbir. Jasbir is now sixteen years of age and about to sit for his GCE examinations at the Ordinary Level. The good Mrs P is able to reconcile her good self to remaining spouse of orderly and temperate shopkeeper who is in the financial department modestly secure only, but only because she can look forward to being also the mother of the famous and so wealthy Jasbir Patel QC, Esq., if not Sir Jasbir at that. I myself am by no means untainted by similar ambition on behalf of our offspring, but I am striving always to prevent such ambitions from becoming overweening. My bones are telling me that overweening ambition unquenched by success is apt to lead to bitterness and unhappiness only, and that success of the requisite order is apt to be in short supply, my friend. But none the less, my deepest wish is that my son can have the kind of success which yours truly, if we are being honest and truthful, was never cut out for.

And I truly believe that Jasbir has it in him to attain such a thing. He is clever and confident and at least some of the good Mrs P's forceful characteristics are born again in him. And he has great advantage over the so long-ago version of yours truly – he is a native-born citizen of old London town and can speak the Queen's English accordingly. If my Jasbir is speaking to you on the telephone, you will not know his name is Patel unless he chooses to tell you so. Indeed, he is perfectly able to convince you if he so wishes that he is native-born citizen of old Belgravia SW1 instead of old Shepherd's Bush only. Not wishing to seem immodest, my friend, but even the good lady wife is admitting said fact as vindication of my own so long-ago decision not to make our home among a community of fellow immigrants, but to give our son instead every chance to grow up as English person. But oh, my friend, it is taking such time and trouble and poor digestion to bring the good lady round to this viewpoint. For years, she is insisting that such notions are merely foolish and that she will only be truly happy in the midst of her own people. I am unable to persuade her that it will be wise to adopt a policy of When in Rome, as she is remaining firmly convinced as long as yours truly is the sole outlet for her overweening ambition that she must in short order return in triumph and riches to her birthplace, there to hold sway over her relations as long as she lives. But she is realist at heart, my friend, and will now confess to me in the privacy of our own domestic circles that she has not been entirely unhappy in our long years here, despite the fears she is originally expressing with such force and vigour. I must tell you, my friend, that the good Mrs P and yours truly will never be completely assimilated as ordinary native-born citizens of old London town, but old London town is nevertheless a place that both of us would be sad to leave. Despite what the papers and the television might have you to believe, my friend, neither I nor any of my small family have ever really encountered what you might term racial prejudice in our lives here. For myself, I am believing that many immigrant complainants of said prejudice are provoking same by their very determination to find it. If one persists in regarding a particular section of the citizenry as one's enemies, said section will be most unlikely to respond in friendly fashion. I try always to behave as if everybody I encounter is my friend already, and I have no enemies known to yours truly.

And as for so-called racial disturbances of the public order, I am inclined to support the views of Dr Heinrich Fischer. 'My dear Patel,' he is saying, 'this is not race behaviour. This is young persons' behaviour, which the tiny minority of active racist persons will naturally seek to turn to their own advantage. Every young person is convinced he has the right to go out and take his happiness from the world by main strength, and if you can but convince him that some party is responsible for keeping his happiness from him, he will go to war with this party. It does not matter whether it is the niggers, or the reds, or the Zoroastrians, or the football supporters of the Nottingham Hotspur, to war he will go.' I am thinking that this is a wise opinion. I am also thinking that should a young white policeman call a young person of any nationality an ape, he will be most unwise to expect him to take it like a man only.

But here we touch on the crux of the matter, my friend, for my Jasbir is now of an age when he himself has the growing tendency towards the most intemperate and disorderly young person's style of behaviour. And if he has learned to speak in the true fashion of old London town, he has learned also to do other things similarly. I am not hidebound traditionalist by any manner or means; I am realizing full well that in allowing my son opportunity to grow up as English person, I must be prepared to take the rough with the smooth, after all is said and done. But when I think of the degree of respect for one's elders and betters which is instilled into yours truly and siblings at a similar tender age, my own son's attitude is shocking, my friend, truly shocking. For not only is my Jasbir less than suitably respectful to his father, it is clear to me that he is taking his father to be foolish only, and that he is thinking himself clever enough to conceal said opinion from yours truly. He is thinking that inability of yours truly and immigrant contemporaries to mingle unremarked in all social respects with native-born citizenry of old London town is infallible sign of our lack of wisdom and general intellectual calibre. And he is further thinking that his own ability to outshine his parent in that particular department is infallible sign likewise of his own superiority in matters of wisdom and judgement. He is so confirmed in this opinion, my friend, that it is now quite beyond the powers of yours truly to convince him otherwise by any manner or means. He is listening, he is putting on a polite face and smiling, he is agreeing with whatever I am telling him, but his eyes are at the same time saying *Yes, yes, poor old fool, but please be getting it over with so I may at once forget it*, and in his heart he does not heed me at all. He counts himself a man already with far more worldly wisdom than yours truly, and his own plans for his immediate future most definitely do not include long hours of study, or even short hours only. He does not, if you please, believe in wasting the best years of one's youth in pursuit of educational qualifications. He does not *believe*, my friend, which is in tantamount to a tragedy. '*Only believe*,' the good Dr Heinrich Fischer is saying often times, 'is good motto indeed, my dear Patel. For how many things of vital importance will cease to function forthwith without the belief of the general populace? Free market economy, communist society, military dictatorship, Halifax Building Society, none will work if general populace does not believe they will work.' And as I say, my friend, I am quite unable to make my Jasbir believe. It is source of deep concern to me, my failure to convince him of the primary necessity of educational success. I fear greatly for his future happiness, because I am sure that in spite of his so many sterling qualities, my Jasbir will never be able to bring his father's so long-ago philosophical attitude to bear upon the menial employment opportunities which will surely be his lot in the absence of GCE at the Ordinary Level. His good lady mother's attitude to the problem I leave to your esteemed imagination, my friend.

Hence the overwhelming importance to yours truly of last night's parents' evening at Jasbir's school. Since the father is now unable totally to reach the heart of the son, the task must fall to the teacher. Mr Baldock who is Jasbir's form teacher is certainly mother-tongue speaker of the Queen's English and a true social adept, and additionally he is professionally qualified person who must surely be commanding respect. Not even the most intemperate and disorderly young person – and my Jasbir is not the worst of his contemporaries in that particular department, by any manner or means – will be thinking himself superior to Mr Baldock in matters of wisdom and judgement. The good Mrs P is impressing upon me in no uncertain terms that yours truly must sally forthwith and impress upon the esteemed Mr Baldock in his turn the vital necessity of convincing our Jasbir of the folly of his ways. It is our last hope, my friend.

Owing to the necessity of personal attendance in the shop to cope with the early evening rush of customers, I am the last in the line of parents waiting their respective turns to interview said Mr Baldock. It has been a most trying day in the shop with many customers in truly unreasonable kidney, and the good lady wife has been particularly fractious also. I am by no means in the best of moods. A person is only human, after all is said and done. And the atmosphere while we are waiting is disconcertingly most disconcertingly like what one experiences at the dental surgery. The other parents waiting ahead of yours truly are all strangers to me, and many of them appear to speak the Queen's English not at all. But I am able none the less to read their feelings with the greatest of ease, my friend, because their feelings are so obviously similar to my own. As in said dental waiting-room, each fears the onset of the unpleasant treatment yet equally is longing for relief said treatment must bring. But as each interview in turn is completed and each interviewed parent is ushered out by said Mr Baldock, it is by no means possible for yours truly to tell whether said treatment has indeed afforded significant measure of said relief. What is more, it is most definitely possible for yours truly to ascertain that Mr Baldock is approaching each forthcoming interview with at least as much apprehension as does each parent. This is truly disconcerting indeed to yours truly, given the nature of my mission. And Mr Baldock's apparent apprehension seems truly justified in the case of the bulky Greek father with the so worried face who is immediately ahead of yours truly. Through the closed door this person can be heard plainly shouting again and again in truly horrendous fashion that his son is lazy no good boy who will disgrace his family and learn nothing unless his teachers beat him and beat him every day. It is not possible to hear what rejoinder Mr Baldock makes to this most vehement assertion, but I am thinking that perhaps said Greek father is in any case not listening, for I am losing count of the number of times he repeats said assertion. At the eventual termination of this so one-sided interview, Mr Baldock is looking most harassed and it is plain that he has quite forgotten that yours truly is still waiting.

45

At the start of our interview, I am giving Mr Baldock pleasant smile to let him know I am by no means about to behave in the fashion of the so worried Greek gentleman, then I am proceeding forthwith to the heart of the matter as the hour is by now quite late. I am explaining most carefully the importance of the issue and just why it is that my son has grown quite unable to heed his father's advice for the reasons aforesaid, et cetera. And I am emphasizing most particularly the key nature of the teacher's role in achieving what aforesaid circumstances render impossible for yours truly. At first, my friend, Mr Baldock is listening with great attentiveness, and I am thinking he is perhaps finding me a blessed relief after the so worried shouting Greek parent and furthermore is taking to heart my most important message. But just as I am coming to the end of my so carefully rehearsed speech, I am truly dumbfounded to observe Mr Baldock lean right back in his chair and commence laughing with great vigour, although the expression on his face is by no means one of amusement. It is taking Mr Baldock quite some time to regain his composure and indeed his breath also in sufficient measure to speak, but at length he is making repeated apologies through the dying throes of his laughing-fit and requests for forgiveness besides. And he is attempting to explain the bitter irony of my so important appeal to him. He is saying that any notion that he or indeed any of his colleagues can command the degree of respect from their pupils in general and my Jasbir in particular which yours truly seems to think only natural is nowadays truly a joke only. He is asking me if problems such as that of my Jasbir's attitude to his studies would be arising in the first place if it were indeed possible for such levels of respect to prevail. And he is asking me, stressing wish not to give offence, what chance the school can have of instilling said respect if the parents are unable to command it in the privacy of their own domestic circles.

It is clear to me that I have failed to make Mr Baldock

understand the very particular reasons for lack of filial respect in the case of Jasbir. Partly, no doubt, this is due to Mr Baldock's being tired and harassed at the end of a fatiguing day, but partly also yours truly has doubtless contributed with his imperfect mastery of the Queen's English. So I am carefully rehearsing the burden of the argument again, being particularly careful to stress key points and to enunciate distinctly also. Alas, this serves only to provoke Mr Baldock in his turn to repeat his own argument, in a more strained and agitated fashion. I am truly perturbed, but the terms of reference dictated to me by the good Mrs P do not permit me to be daunted. I am taking great care to keep the stiff upper lip, I am firmly resisting any temptation to become irritable, I am explaining said points yet again with even more emphasis and clarity. Mr Baldock, instead of appreciating what is after all a fairly simple message, is looking at yours truly in most peculiar way and then launching into yet another repetition of his own statement, only this time delivered in the manner of a person with some truly horrendous psychiatric disorder. I am at a loss. I interrupt him most politely but firmly. I begin again with yet more care and emphasis. To my horror, I perceive Mr Baldock regard me as if he fears I will fall impromptu twitching to the floor frothing at the mouth and, oh dear me, he now breaks in on me again with truly stupendous brusqueness and aggression. Mr Baldock has plainly become unhinged totally. All that is stopping yours truly from summoning assistance is puzzling fact that Mr Baldock clearly thinks exactly the same about yours truly.

A light is dawning upon me.

I am bursting out with laughter which makes Mr Baldock's own earlier outbreak appear feeble only. I am eventually able to restrain said laughter only by reflecting that Mr Baldock will surely take it to be further evidence of my lunacy.

I am explaining matters to Mr Baldock. He is joining me in laughter.

We do not solve the said immediate problem of my son Jasbir, but Mr Baldock and I part as friends.

What I am explaining to Mr Baldock is as follows. In the undoubted heat of the moment, yours truly is forgetting most of his so long-ago observations and meditations on the Queen's English. Unable to think clearly owing to stressful circumstances, I am in part reverting to habits of speaking and listening more appropriate to that treacherously similar long-ago tongue which is so near to and yet so far from the Queen's English. Such a small difference, but enough. When I wish to emphasize a point, I naturally do so in this long-ago language by raising both the volume and musical pitch of my voice and I tend to speak more rapidly also, with frequent repetition of key words and phrases orchestrated with vigorous emphatic gestures of the hands. All of which I mean to emphasize only, but to a Queen's English listener such as Mr Baldock it is evident that yours truly is becoming deranged, yes? And a Queen's English speaker such as Mr Baldock, my friend, he will naturally emphasize his argument by speaking more clearly and ultimately in staccato fashion with totally separate words enunciated in a flat unemotional tone. I shall give you three guesses, my friend, what an unthinking listener in my long-ago so-near-and-yet-so-far tongue will take for signs of incipient madness in his interlocutor.

As I have said, none of this solves my Jasbir problem, by any manner or means. But in a way which yours truly does not pretend to understand, it helps to solve the immediate good Mrs P problem. I am so buoyed up by the happy outcome of the interview with Mr Baldock that I am able to persuade the good lady wife to see things in the same light as yours truly. Oh yes, my friend, such things happen. Once or twice a year, they happen. I am able to persuade her that matters are not so black, perhaps, as we have thought, and that it is necessary at all costs to look upon the bright side. All young men of Jasbir's age go through such a phase, after all is

said and done. With a positive attitude, much can be ac-
complished in the most disheartening circumstances. 'The
past,' the good Dr Heinrich Fischer is often saying, 'is not
necessarily good guide to the future, which consists of stuff
that didn't happen yet.' I shall make a gesture of faith in the
future, I am telling Mrs P. Tomorrow I shall plant in our small
garden an apple tree. Only a true optimist can sensibly plant
a tree, my friend.

FIREWORK NIGHT ISN'T IN IT

For Mary Pryor

He says to her, he says, 'I am an innocent man and I have been martyred.' He does, he says it twenty times a day. 'I have been crucified,' he says to her. 'Yes, flower,' she says to him, ''course you have, flower.' He is my half-uncle, Tim is. My father was Tim's half-brother. Tim has always been very good to me, Tim has. In the old days, before it all happened, she would have a go at him and buck him up. Madeline, that is, she being Tim's wife. I don't know if that makes her my half-aunt and in fact I am not sure if it is really proper to call Tim my half-uncle, but they always said to not call them anything and just Tim and Madeline will do fine, Vera, so the case do not come up. But the way Tim is now it will not do no good to have a go at him and buck him up, and Madeline knows that so she leaves it out. It is an utter disgust and a totally reprobate step what they done to Tim and left him the way he is. Tim and Madeline are the both of them not a lot older than me and you might think that's funny with me being their half-niece, but it can quite easy happen if you think about it.

When I first came to live with Tim and Madeline, it was a really nice little home life we had here. They was the both of them really nice to me. And I was ever so grateful, of course, but they would never even let me give them a thank-you, not neither one of them. It was a bit on the lonely side for them in the evening before I came, mind, with not having no children and them not getting no younger. Especially Tim, with his condition. And then their cat had died; thirteen years old, that cat. They wouldn't never have another one. But even so.

They made me welcome right away. I come here when Dad

died. I looked after my old dad for seventeen years, you know. By myself; he wouldn't let no one else in the house after Mother went, not even the doctor or the man to read the electric. I always had to fill out one of them postcards they put through the door with the little clock-pictures on and stick it to the front room window for the electric man to see. Dad had to show me how to fill it out at first, of course. I can't read or write, you see. They tell me a lot of people would consider that a handicap and be ashamed to admit it, and they always say to me about how wonderful it is that I'm not ashamed to admit it. I don't understand that. I can't ride a bike, neither, or knit, but no one ever says how wonderful it is I'm not ashamed to admit that.

I never had a job at all before I come here, not one where they paid you. Dad was a full-time job after Mother went, but that's not the same thing, is it? Not that *he* ever paid me nothing. I didn't actually come to Tim and Madeline looking for no job, of course. I just come to them for a roof over my head. They wouldn't let me keep the house on after Dad went, they said I had to get out, and I didn't have nobody else to turn to. I've always been an only child, you see, and I couldn't really make myself no friends with Dad the way he was, could I? Someone was saying in the shop a while back that they changed the law about that now, where they got to let the children keep the lease up when their parent dies, but that come too late for me. And I don't understand about the law much anyway, except that it always seems to go against them as least deserves it, which is part of the trouble. Me not understanding the law, that is. But what I meant to say to you was they had me here because I was family, no other reason. Very good to me they was, the both of them.

Looking back on it, I don't think I was ever really happy before I come to Tim and Madeline. You might even say I had a miserable old time of it as a young woman. After Mother's legs went, I had no life to call my own, and the best years of your life as well. I used to be in a despair about it. A young person very easy gets into a despair about that sort of thing, don't you? It is always a surprise to me that more young people don't make off with themselves over getting into a despair. But when you get a bit older, you find out it's not the end of the world, whatever it is that's putting the despair on you, don't you? And I've always been able to fall back on the faith, of course. Religion has always been ever such a comfort to me. It is like the laws of the Swedes and the Persians, which altereth not neither does it change. I think of some of the young people that have come in the shop over the years with their funny hair and health-food clothes and you could see the despair on them. I wanted to say to them to just wait a few years or better still to get yourself a faith to fall back on, but that would be too forward, to say a thing like that to anyone. And I often think now that Tim and Madeline would bear their present cross ever so much better if they had a faith to fall back on, but they are neither one of them religious at all. I would never dream of blaming them for that, of course. It is just the ways of the times we live in.

When I first come to live here, Tim struck me as ever such a *wise* soul, despite him not being at all religious. He was so full of things to say. 'You're all right with a nice steady little chemist's shop, Vera,' he would say, 'good times and bad times, people are always going to get sick and want the doctor and the chemist. And even if they don't get sick, most of them will want to spend money to stay well. Plus you always have the photographic.' It turned out in the end he was wrong there, about always having a steady trade, but he did make it sound ever so *wise*. He was ever so sensible, Tim was. People would come in the shop and see Tim with their aches and pains rather than go to the doctor because Tim was so sensible, and this was years after the National Health and such so it wasn't the money. 'When you are young, Vera,' Tim would say, 'when you're young and you never have enough of anything to be really comfortable, all you want to do is go all out and make yourself all the money you can as fast as you can. Only natural. You think the money's going to make you feel secure and happy, don't you? Let you relax. But when you've been around long enough, Vera, you find there's a limit to how much better more money makes you feel. Too much money doesn't make you secure; it makes you a target. Much better off with a nice steady little chemist's shop. Nobody ever comes in a shotgun gang to rob a nice steady little chemist's shop.' I don't know why Tim ever bothered to go talking to me about money and such; I never did have no head for none of that. Madeline would have a go at him if she heard him talking that way, but it was just in fun.

'You wouldn't believe he would ever say such things if you knew the man I married, Vera,' she would say to me but meant for him, really. 'The man I married was such a goer. Going to make a name for himself, Vera, going to the top. If he was a hairdresser, he wouldn't have rested until he outdone Egon Ronay, or do I mean Gore Vidal? Whatever happened to the man I married, Vera?' 'Time,' Tim used to say, 'time happened to him.' He knew she was just having a go at him to buck him up.

Tim is a thin little man with silver hair and glasses, and he looks no different to me from when I moved in here. He walks with a stick and sometimes his hand shakes, but otherwise you could never tell about his condition. Tim has that multiple whatsit, I never could get my tongue around it. Always ever so brave about that, Tim was.

It turned out in the end he was wrong about the chemist's never being robbed and all. When the kids first started taking all them pills, they was forever having to repair our back window where they was in and out all the time helping themselves. Tim had to put in steel bars and a dog in the finish, only the dog died young. I wonder do they break in the ironmonger's now for glue to sniff? And when they done that squat in the end house, just past the greengrocer and the While-U-Wait shoe repairs with Keys Cut and Unisex Ear-piercing that's gone bust now, well. Nobody was sacred with them around. Scruff of the earth, they were. Did you hear where they interviewed them on the radio that time? Educated people they seemed to be, plenty to say for themselves. You could still tell, mind, you could tell in their heart they were dead common, eat with their mouth full and that. But all this was much later, of course. I get so mixed up. When you grow old, your memory of things gets ever so clear some of the time, but it can be a real job to sort out what happened before what else.

It was Tim first said to me about doing a little job in the shop. He said it would be company for me instead of sitting alone upstairs all the time. When I first come here, Tim and Madeline didn't have no help at all except for the Saturday girl, and it takes at least two when the shop's busy. You need someone behind the counter while Tim's doing up the pre-scriptions. So I used to be sat alone upstairs quite a lot through the day. I couldn't go out for a walk much because I was a stranger to the area and I very easy get lost in a strange place. I didn't want to be a nuisance to Tim and Madeline with a policeman forever bringing me home lost. And Tim was right in a way about being alone. There has never been a telly in this house, you see, Tim is very down on the telly. And I never did get on with just the sound radio. The plays would always make me nervous with all those *sounds* and nothing to look at. And music – well, to me music is just some noises that some people happen to like, but I'm not one of them. So I was only too glad to help out downstairs when Tim said to me about it.

Two pounds a week, that was what he paid me. Tim was ever so fair about it. 'If you do not think that's enough, Vera, you just say so and I'll have a little think to see if the business can run to any more.' I never had that much money of my own in my hand at the one time before. There was the Post Office book, of course, but that all went in a few shillings at a time, and in any case it was only for a rainy day. Dad was ever so strict about that when he was alive. He would inspect the bank book every time I paid in to make sure they done right by me down the Post Office. I tried to get Tim to have some of that Post Office money for my keep when I first come here, but he wouldn't. 'It's not a rainy day yet, Vera,' he said.

I really enjoyed that little job in the shop. It was strange at first, of course, but Tim and Madeline were very good over showing me how all the different bottles and packets and things looked. I could always stick my head around the door of the dispensary and ask Tim if I wasn't sure, and customers are mostly very good too. They are only too pleased to help if you ask them nicely if they want this packet or is it that one?

I did about half the counter time myself at first, the times when Tim would be too busy to come out the dispensary. Madeline and Tim used to divide up the rest of the time between the two of them, the times when just the one person could manage. They didn't want me to have to do it all on my own until I had a bit of experience, see? 'Don't you worry over it, Vera,' Tim would say, 'all it takes is a bit of time and experience to build up the confidence. There's plenty of time for that, no hurry.' And he was right, as usual. Him and Madeline was ever so patient and kind with me, and it didn't seem like no time at all before they had me trained up to where I could manage the shop all on my own when it was quiet. I was so grateful to them for being so patient and kind. It was a revelation to me that people could be so kind; my Dad was never what you could call a kind man, though he had been sorely tried, mind. Tim and Madeline showed me how you could find a goodness in people, even if they are in no way religious, in just ordinary people.

It was really useful for Tim and Madeline for me to be able to manage in the shop, and I was ever so pleased to be able to pay them something back for being so good to me. Madeline had more time free to do the shopping and the house and Tim had more time free to do the books and such instead of sitting at them after hours. And the both of them could get away for a little break together now and then. 'I know we used to manage without you before you came, Vera,' Madeline would say, 'but I don't know that I could ever go back to that now. You are a real treasure to us, you really are.' I'm sure she believed it was good for Tim's condition, to have a little break every now and again. She is ever such a chatty person, Madeline. She would be forever telling me stories in the shop about their young days, just chatting to pass the time. She would say about when Tim first came courting her and he was working giving driving lessons in them days, out of his own little car. And Madeline's father was a bit of a one and he would always take the rise out of Tim just to keep him in his place. He liked Tim, but he wouldn't let on because he didn't want him getting above his place. And he would tease him about the permanent L-plates on his car and Tim was only young and took it ever so serious. And he made this long solemn speech about it being good for advertising but of course, sir, you're right in a way and perhaps it would be more dignified to cover them up when on private business, and Madeline and her sister fit to burst trying not to laugh. She would tell me where Tim would take her and her sister out driving into the country, and once he took them to a cricket match. He smuggled them into the beer tent even though Madeline and her sister was under age, and he got them all a bit squiffy. And when they was watching the cricket afterwards it was a bit boring, so Tim started calling out, 'Hand ball!' every time someone picked the ball up. Everyone was trying to see who was doing the shouting, but Tim was ever so good at that whatsit, that dummy stuff without moving your lips, so they couldn't none of them be sure it was him. 'How we laughed about it in the car afterwards, Vera,' Madeline would say, 'we laughed and laughed and laughed! You know how young people can laugh, Vera.' Actually, I didn't have much cause to know about laughing when I was young myself, but I did so love to listen to Madeline chatting that I never said to her about it.

And in the evenings, after I did the washing-up, we would all of us sit together in the front room and maybe have a game of ludo or just sit around and listen to Tim talk. Madeline wasn't nearly so chatty if Tim was there, but that was just because Tim was such a lovely talker to listen to. 'I see where they are saying in the paper it is time for us Englishmen to stand up and be counted,' he might say. 'Well, I refuse to stand up and be counted. Who wants to be a number?' He was ever so wise, Tim was. 'I don't want to own no Rolls Royce,' he would say, 'because I don't want the neighbours to take me for a chauffeur. I do not cut the figure to be taken for no Rolls Royce owner.' He would always give you little bits of advice about your life, too, and if he thought you'd forgot them he'd give them to you again. Ever so thoughtful, Tim was. 'You want to steer clear of the old legal beavers,' he would tell us. 'Don't ever get mixed up with them. A lawyer will have your all, girls. Stay clear of the legal beavers.' That is one thing where Tim definitely turned out to be right in the end, I must say. But he did so enjoy talking to us. 'I do so enjoy talking to you, girls,' he once said, 'you are so interesting to talk to.' 'Good listeners mostly are, flower,' Madeline says to him. A really nice little home life, we used to have here.

I never used to go out of doors at all, hardly, but I never felt the lack. I was too busy with all the things to do during the day, and only too glad to sit still of an evening. I used to go out to Church twice of a Sunday, of course, it being quite easy to find after Madeline took me there the first time. But it was always on my own to Church, with Tim and Madeline the way they was. I would have been ever so pleased for them to come to Church with me, mind, but I never said to them about it because that would be too forward. I was never out with Tim and Madeline but the once in all the years I lived here, you know. Tim is very steady in his ways as a rule, but every so often he does take a whim to do something different. Madeline never stands in his way when he takes a whim; I think she doesn't like to cross him due to his condition. And this one time Tim took a whim that I was to go with them when they went up West to do the museums. That was a great favourite of Tim and Madeline's, doing the museums. They very often done that in later years, but they never had me along before Tim took this whim. 'It is a celebration, Vera,' he says, 'it is our twenty years anniversary. You have been with us twenty years this week, Vera.' I never realized that till Tim said it, but he was quite right. The time goes ever so quickly when you get to a certain age. I didn't really want to go with them, you know, being what you might call set in my ways, but I couldn't disappoint Tim no more than Madeline could, so I went.

Well, the bus ride alone was nearly enough to finish me, being so unused to it, but Tim bought us all a nice little lunch in this cafeteria place, and I felt ever so much better after that. Tim said we would do the Geological first, it being a calmer sort of place and less likely to upset me, also not so crowded. He was right, too; it was a clean and quiet and respectable place where nobody talked too loud, just like in a great big church. After we spent a bit of time looking at the precious stones in the glass cases, I felt quite at home. So Tim asked me if I felt up to a bit of excitement, and I said yes, and he took us into this little room where they had a display about earthquakes, pictures on a big screen and a voice telling you all about it. And at the finish of the display, the voice said this is what it feels like to be in an earthquake of such and such a strength, and I was wondering what they meant, and then the floor started to shake and jerk. They had the floor rigged to some machine, you see, to show you what it felt like. I could

see Tim and Madeline watching me to see how I was taking
it, but I was quite all right, really, knowing it was just a
machine. Tim was ever so pleased and telling me that was the
spirit, Vera, and then he took us on a little tour around these
other displays they had. He was ever so good about trying to
explain it to me, Tim was, but I must admit it was mostly over
my head. Like a foreign language, really. It mostly seemed to
be about how the middle of the world is full of a molten fiery
furnace that makes real earthquakes and bursts out through
volcanoes in foreign parts and sometimes America too. That
was a bit of an uncomfortable thing to think about, it not
being just a machine as it were, but the hard bit on the top
where we live is miles and miles thick. Besides, you don't
really get volcanoes and such round here, do you?

And then Tim showed me the football. They had a glass
case with an ordinary white football in it, and there was a
stamp stuck on the football. It looked to be a first-class stamp
and not franked, but I couldn't see no address on the football
at all. 'What do you make of that, Vera,' says Tim, but I
couldn't make head nor tail of it. And then he told me that if
the whole world was the size of that football, then the molten
fiery furnace would be as big as the white ball and the hard
bit on the outside where we live would be as thick as the
stamp. 'And it's hell in there, Vera,' he says. That was when I
was took funny and they had to get me home in a taxi and my
nerves was so bad I was laid up for a week. I never really
fancied going out with Tim and Madeline after that.

I first seen Bella when she come in the shop. It was the
second or third time she come in that I noticed her properly;
what I noticed was that she perhaps would become a regular
customer because she'd been in more than the once. In a
chemist's shop, some of your customers might only come in a
couple of times a year, but we've all been here that long we'd
still call them regulars. And I was on the look-out for new
regulars due to the shop being very slack, of course. This was

a little while after they opened the new shopping centre and they had a Boots *and* an Underwoods, which hit the shop very bad. Tim was always having a grumble about it and you could see that he was ever so worried, and I don't think it was doing his condition no good, either.

As I say, I first noticed Bella in the shop, but I first met her properly at All Hallows. Bella is the first completely new regular face I can remember at All Hallows for years and years; a complete stranger, I mean, not just somebody's children growing up or the people they marry. She come up to me outside after the service and she said, 'I *do* hope you won't think me rude, but I'm *sure* I know your face from somewhere and I can't think of it for the life of me.' I says to her, I says, 'Small bottle of Murine', and she looked at me very funny and then she laughed. 'Red and blue bottles,' she says, 'the old-fashioned chemist with the big red and blue bottles in the window. My mother used to take me into a chemist with bottles like that in the window when I was little.' Bella is about – I don't know, really, so difficult to judge a young person's age these days, don't you find? Say thirty. She was walking in my direction anyway, and she turned out to be ever such a pleasant person to talk to, or listen to, really, her being a bit of a chatterbox. She was saying about how she had a job in that Council advice place in the shopping centre and she first started coming in the shop in her lunch hour, but now the Council had got her a flat local so that was why she'd started at All Hallows. Ever so friendly, she was. Do you know, in all the years I have been going to that church, Bella is the only person who ever really tried to talk to me properly? Not just politeness, I mean? It's a nice little church on the inside even if the outside could do with some mending, but everybody has always had our own personal seat, and being so few of us we're too far apart to do much more than smile and nod. I never really *met* any of the other people even though I always looked forward so much to seeing them every week. And with Bella, she makes you feel straight away that you've been a friend all your lives.

Pretty soon Bella was popping in the shop nearly every day to see me. She would always buy a little something, maybe some tissues or a toothpaste, but it was really to see me and have a chat. Tim would sometimes get a bit irritated at the time Bella would take up chatterboxing, but he never said to her about it, of course. 'In the retail trade, Vera,' Tim has said to me time and again, 'in the retail trade you have to be prepared to be nice to *everybody*. It has got to be part of your stock in trade.' Besides which she was spending some money and the shop was very slack. Bella would tell me all about when she was little and about the people who would come in the advice place and about how her husband split up with her and a good thing too, and anything that came into her head, really. Thinking about it now, I can see where Bella was maybe a bit of a lonely person herself and looking for company to talk to, but I didn't see that at all at the time. I was just pleased that someone would take such an interest in me and talk to me, someone not family like Tim and Madeline, I mean. In the shop, the people who wanted to chat generally wanted to chat about their aches and pains, and that meant talking to Tim, not me, of course. I was left out of it in the shop till Bella come.

We became real good friends, Bella and me. I used to say to her about being old enough to be her mother, but she would just laugh and say as how a girl's best friend is her mother. She really did bring me out of myself. I would not be talking to you like this now if it was not for Bella. Of course, I wouldn't have nothing to tell you about if it was not for Bella, but you know what I mean. It was her who first got me to notice that I never really talked to anyone outside Tim and Madeline. She used to take ever such an interest in me. Besides All Hallows and the shop, she started to take me out of an evening for a little outing. We would just go for a walk and maybe listen to the music in the park, or sometimes we would go to the pictures. Do you know, I hadn't been to the pictures since before Mother went? I had very nearly forgotten what it was like. Tim and Madeline never went in for the pictures, but they were very pleased to see me start going again. 'It *is* good to see you with a friend all your own, Vera,' Madeline would say. When I was all dressed up ready to go out with Bella, Tim would say, 'Doesn't she look smart? Doesn't she look *sartorial*?'

Actually, I never liked to say to Tim about it, but I had all these clothes the whole time I been with them, a whole wardrobe of clothes I made myself when I was still with Dad. But I never had any call to wear most of them before, except those suitable for indoors work or for Church. Do you know, I can still get into dresses I made myself at twenty? When you look at what the young ones wear over the years, some of my dresses have been high fashion two or three times. I have scarcely needed to buy a thing to wear since I came here, there still being bolts and bolts of good cloth in my chests to run up if need be. Did I tell you Dad was in the textile line? Our cellar was always chock-full of oddments he couldn't bring himself to part with. I would gladly have run up anything for Madeline at any time if she wanted, but she never said to me about it. 'I'm ever so impressed, Vera,' Bella says to me when I told her about making my own dresses, 'I'm hopeless; can't even thread a needle.' But I told her not to worry over what you can't do, because I can't knit at all myself, but just you give me a sewing machine. And Bella said about how I should have had a career in fashion, but it's no use crying over spilt milk. I used to say about that to Bella when she would make a fuss about me not being able to read and write. Bella was ever so concerned about that when she found out, ever so sympathetic. She said she expected it was a case of dyswhatsit, some medical thing I couldn't get my tongue round. I must say I never thought of it as medical, but

Bella is a very educated sort of person, as is only right in her line of work.

I really do owe Bella such a lot despite what happened; I would never want anyone to think I was not grateful to Bella. Tim and Madeline have both turned bitter towards her and they tell each other it was her whole plan from the very start, but that is just their own bad feelings leading them astray. Bella was only after my own best interests, plus the law of the land. Anyone not led astray by their own bad feelings could always see that she never had no arterial motives at all.

How it first came up, I needed some cash to pay for the pictures. It being my turn, I mean. Bella and me have this little system where we take turn and turn about to pay for both the two tickets. It saves a little bit of time for everybody in the queue, although there very often isn't enough people to have a real queue at the early show me and Bella usually go to. And it does make it seem more of a sociable sort of thing if the one person pays for both the two tickets, do you know what I mean? In the normal way, I would make sure in advance I had the money. I would go with Tim or Madeline when they went out shopping or to the bank. They would come in the Post Office with me and check that the bank book was done up right. I always use that little blue Post Office on the corner with the haberdashers and knitting wool combined. Such a pleasant man that runs it, that nice Mr Patel, though I do wish he wouldn't burn those joss things that smell like incense. We had a new vicar a couple of years before Dad died and he was ever so High; he started having incense and all sorts. It put Dad right off. He said it was Romish and an utter disgust and the morning service on the radio would do him till things were sorted, which they never was of course. Such a pity; I'm sure Dad would have gone much easier if he had still been a regular churchgoer. I'm glad to say we have always been very Low at All Hallows, no smells except the cut flowers and sometimes a whiff of Pledge. But what I meant to say was I'm sure that nice Mr Patel would never do my bank book up wrong, not on a purpose, no more his wife neither. Such a nice woman, though she never speaks to you, such a nice smile. But I never feel right unless I get someone to check the book for me, so I had to get Bella to do it on the way to the pictures. And so she couldn't very well help seeing, could she?

She never said to me about it straight away, though I did notice she was ever so thoughtful-looking on the way to the pictures and not her usual chatty self at all. She said to me about it when we were having a coffee and an ice in the pizza place afterwards. 'I hope you will not think I am prying, Vera,' she says to me, 'but I couldn't help seeing in your bank how you always pay in exactly eight pounds every week.' So I explained to her how this was my wages from the shop, after taking out the two 50ps for Church collections. I always put my money in the Post Office for a rainy day, with not really having to spend anything except if it's my turn for the pictures. And Bella says she'd thought as much, and then she asked me ever so many questions about what hours I did and days off and holidays, and contracts of this and conditions of that and a lot of other stuff over my head, but I did my best to answer it for Bella. Well, you would, wouldn't you? For a friend taking such an interest in you, I mean. I must say, she took it ever so seriously and she was writing away in that fat notebook with the pink cat on the cover that she always carries at the top of her bag. When she finished asking questions, she had a little think, then she ordered us another coffee and she sort of made me a little speech, if you know what I mean. I was thinking this was how she must be when she's being official in the advice place. You could tell she was trying ever so hard to make me see what she was saying, but I'm afraid an awful lot still went over my head. She was saying about this law and that law and minimum wages and tribunals and contracts of I don't know what. In the end, I got properly flustered and I thought I was going to be took funny like that time in the Geological. But Bella can be ever such a soothing person and she got me to calm down. She would insist that I got the message, though, which was that Tim might be breaking such a lot of laws over my little job in the shop. 'I am the last one to cause trouble for a friend, Vera,' she says to me, 'but you really must speak to Tim about it. In his own interests as well as yours.' And she made me promise.

I hope you don't think from me talking to you like this that I am a forward sort of person. I am not at all like that, not even after Bella got me to come out of myself a bit more. I was really dreading saying to Tim about what Bella said, but a promise is a promise. But even in my worst dreading, I never imagined Tim would take on so. I was afraid Tim might think I was being ungrateful, which was never the case with me as I hope and pray I have made plain to you. I had no grumble about the wages; Tim put them up every so often without me even having to ask. And as for days off and holidays, well. What would I want with holidays? I was always content with my little job and in no way ungrateful. It was just the idea of being against the law that made me say to Tim about it. And the promise, of course.

I expect I muddled it up a bit when I said it to him the first time, what with the dreading and everything, plus I was never absolutely sure of everything Bella told me about it. Tim made me go over it again, anyway, and he was looking more and more poorly the whole time we was talking. In the end he had to sit down, he was shaking that much with his condition. He sat quiet and thoughtful for a little bit, and then he started on me. I don't mean he shouted and roared at me the way Dad used to. I mean he was begging and pleading with me in a little quiet voice and with tears rolling down his cheeks so I didn't know where to put myself. Saying about didn't I realize how low the business was and the property mortgaged over their heads and all their savings pumped into the shop to keep their heads above water, not like me with my life savings untouched for a rainy day? And talk about a rainy day, didn't I know it had been a blankety-blank down-pour for the shop ever since that blankety-blank shopping centre opened up? That is the only time in twenty years I ever heard Tim use *language*, and even then he never raised his voice to me. And he was going on and on and saying to me about how could I do this to my own flesh and blood and hadn't they always done the right thing by me and what kind of gratitude was this and what would become of us all put out on the street at our age and the tears rolling and rolling down his face. It was far worse than any shouting and roaring, far far worse. And in the finish I really *was* took funny like in the Geological, only ever so bad. I hope and pray you never feel as poorly as I felt then, I hope and pray it. I was laid up for days afterwards, completely prostrated. And Tim was left with his condition worse than ever and poor Madeline was left to do the shop on her own and it's a mercy trade was so slack, with the two of us for her to nursemaid besides.

After a couple of days, Bella come in the shop to see me and her and Madeline had this terrible row. I could hear them all the way upstairs, their voices but not the words, so they must have been really shouting. Tim got up and started to go downstairs when he heard, but he was shaking so bad he never got no further than the chair on the landing. When Madeline came upstairs afterwards she was shaking nearly as bad as Tim – only for temper, not from no condition. 'That woman!' she says to him, 'That *woman*!', but then it sounded like she forced herself to shut up so as not to upset Tim any worse. 'She'll be the end of us,' Tim says to Madeline on the landing, 'she'll be the end of us or I am a double-Dutch uncle.' 'You just go and lie down again, flower,' Madeline says to him. She could tell even then it was no good no more having a go at him to buck him up.

But it didn't end there. Bella was back the very next day.

She brought some man from the Council with her and she didn't go through the shop; she come to the front door of the flat, which is on the side. Tim's shaking was a bit better by then and he was down the stairs and let them in before Madeline could stop him. I could hear Bella talking to Tim and the Council man's voice, too, and then Madeline come up the other stairs from the shop and met them on the landing. And Madeline really started to have a go at them only it was not at all in fun. I think she only kept herself from really screaming and shouting to not upset Tim, but you could still hear how angry she was. She said to Bella to get out and never darken her door, and how dare she come interfering with her husband not a well man and poor Vera prostrated with her nerves because of her interference. And she said to the poor Council man to get out instead of standing round looking like best man at a funeral, to get out and do some proper work to earn the honest ratepayers' good money. But Bella is not a person you can very easily daunt. She said how they was not content with exploiting me for years; they was now holding me a prisoner and she insisted on seeing me, insisted. And then Madeline really did start screaming and shouting and they had this terrible terrible row, and then Bella and the Council man went away again. The whole time I wanted to get up and tell them it was all so stupid, such a stupid thing to think, but I couldn't manage it, I was so prostrated I just couldn't.

A prisoner? Me, a prisoner? How could Bella ever think such a thing? Looking back I think maybe meeting all the low types who go in the advice place has warped Bella's mind a bit and soured her view of human nature. But I will still insist that she had my best interests in her heart.

Well, a little bit after that the summons come registered post. I was up and about by this time though still not too clever, and Tim was back serving in the shop for short spells. When they got the summons, though, he was back worse than ever with his condition. 'She will do for us,' he would say, again and again, 'that woman is determined to have her pound of flesh and blood, Mad.' 'Don't upset yourself, flower,' Madeline would tell him. And she would say to me about not to upset myself neither, having been led sadly astray just like her and Tim. 'You were not to know she would be a viper in your bosom, Vera,' she would say, 'you were not to know she would be a rattlesnake in the grass.' I wanted to tell Tim and Madeline they were all wrong over Bella, but I could see the both of them had their hearts and minds set on being down on her. I had a sense that it would be a terrible upset to them to try and change their hearts and minds, so I never said to them about it.

The court business was supposed to be all right, you know. It was all supposed to be arranged. I prayed and prayed it would all go all right in court for Tim. I find that prayer will make you feel better even if it doesn't make anything happen, don't you? Tim would never have any truck with lawyers, not at the best of times, but this inspector of something chap and one of his assistants came round to explain things. They wanted Tim to get himself a lawyer, but Tim wouldn't do it. So they explained it to Tim what he was supposed to do by this law and that law if he was employing a person full-time, and in the finish Tim had to say to them that he supposed he must be breaking the law, though what do they expect if they have such damn fool laws and don't tell people about it? And the inspector chap said to Tim to just explain to the tribunal that it was all an honest mistake and it should be all right, even though the law is still the law. And he said if Tim would be pleading guilty, I would not need to attend court with my health and it would be enough to swear out an affywhatsit. So the assistant put down what I said on a legal paper and read it out to me, and I put a cross at the bottom and they wrote their names as well.

Tim and Madeline seemed to be feeling a bit better in

71

themselves after this, though it was still not a good idea to bring up Bella's name with them. And when Tim come back after the court thing, he seemed quite relieved. He looked as though a weight had been lifted from him, a great weight. Madeline couldn't hardly wait for him to tell us about it. She couldn't go to the court place herself, you see, due to the shop. I was up and about myself by this time, of course, going out for the odd little walk and such, but I still wasn't quite up to the shop and somebody had to see to it. 'I don't know how to put it, Mad,' Tim says to her, 'I don't know how to tell it to you. I went in there feeling like when you're sent to see the Headmaster in school. You know, when you *know* he's going to think you've done something, no matter what you say, because otherwise why would you have got sent to him? I was expecting it to be fierce judges in wigs, all stern, and browbeating trick questions with spikes round the edge of the dock to make you feel beaten before you start. But it wasn't a bit like that. They were all very nice, I must say. They could see I was a bit nervous, and they were all very nice to me. There was this young chap in a dark suit, very well spoken and polite. I'm not sure if he was a lawyer or what; nobody told me. But he very kindly helped me explain everything to the tribunal; you know, kind of led me through it step by step and made helpful suggestions when I was at a loss for a word, that sort of thing. And the others sometimes asked questions as well if they weren't sure. I did what the inspector chap said and I told them I was sorry if I'd broken any regulations and taken up their valuable time, but I didn't know I was doing anything wrong. Then they told me I'd broken this law and that law, and that ignorance of the law had never been a valid defence and in any case there were leaflets available. And then they fined me, Mad. But they gave me time to pay and they weren't at all nasty about it. I felt – oh, I don't know what I felt. I think I felt disappointed, Mad.' Then Madeline said to him not to take on, flower, and to have a sit down and a nice cup of tea, and I thought the court business had all gone like it was supposed to be arranged.

So when the young lady spoke to me in the park a couple of days later, I thought she was just being friendly. Well, you would, wouldn't you? She sat down beside me in the tea place and we got chatting and I was telling her about how I usually come with my friend Bella, only there'd been a falling-out. Not with me and Bella, but between Bella and my relatives. And I told her the half-uncle thing, and she *did* laugh! And it just sort of carried on from there, really, and pretty soon I'd told her everything there was to tell. I gave her the photo, too, the one of me and Tim and Madeline outside the shop that Bella took that time. The young lady did seem ever so interested and I never did like that photo; it makes me look sort of vacant and I only ever kept it so as to not hurt Bella's feelings. I never did take a good photo. But honestly, I really did think the young lady was just being friendly. I didn't know there'd been a bit about Tim's court business in the evening paper, did I? I wasn't to know she was from one of the Sunday papers. Even when things were at their worst afterwards and Tim was at his lowest, Madeline still said to me about how was I to know and to not go blaming yourself, Vera.

But it was bad enough, for all that. I was washing and Madeline was wiping when we heard Tim shout out in the front room. No words, that is, just the awful shout. Madeline dropped a plate and ran straight through. I couldn't go after her straight away, having to dry my hands first so as to not make drips and then sweep up the broken plate or someone might have an accident. When I did get there, she was still trying to get him to tell her what was the matter. 'What is it, flower?' she was saying to him, 'Tell me what it is.' But he just sat there with his mouth open and these awful baby noises coming out his throat. He was making little struggling moves with his two hands in front of him like he was helping

73

Madeline ball her wool. I thought he'd had a stroke like Dad's first one that left him with his speech all funny and I was thinking what a terrible thing for Tim to go and have on top of his condition and everything. But then it was like his one hand broke free from something holding it back, and he let out another awful shout and slammed his fist down on the paper spread out in front of him.

You could tell he was upset.

He made the whole dining table jump, and he has always had only a small hand on him, Tim. He pushed the paper at Madeline and made with his hands for her to read. That's when I saw the photo, the photo I gave the lady in the park, and it come to me that she must have really been someone from the paper. But I never had no chance to say about it because Madeline was going stark raging mad. She was white in the face and shaking and so angry she could not get her words properly. 'That! How dare – ?' she was saying, 'Just you! Oh, I shall – ! The gall. Oh! She!' Maybe that sounds silly to you now but to me it sounded really frightening, the way she was saying it. She sounded ready to do blue murder and at the same time you could hear she was still trying to hold herself in. To not upset Tim, perhaps, or even me. She didn't read none of the paper out loud and you couldn't tell from her broken-up words what it was really saying in the paper, except that it was something very bad. And you couldn't tell who it was that Madeline was so angry at; the paper lady or Bella or me or even herself.

When she got a proper control of herself, Madeline sort of shooshed me out of the room and tried to tell me there was nothing for me to be concerned about. I could tell that wasn't true, but I thought best not to say to her about it in that mood. To this day, neither Tim nor Madeline has said a blind word to me about anything it said in that paper. And even though I am by no means a prying sort of person, you can't help but noticing that it has broken up the both of their lives for them.

Madeline goes through the day in the shop like she was not really there; you never hear her having a chat nowadays. And as for Tim – well, I already told you the way he has been left. Our old home life that we used to have of an evening seems like another world now. I even have a dee of a job to get out to meet Bella without them knowing and going off into a paddy, which will only leave them even worse if it happens. It's funny when you think of the way things used to be, but I am left the only one with any go in them, and that can't say a lot for the others, can it?

I had a dream about my old Dad last night. I don't hardly ever have any dreams I remember about, but I remembered this one. It was after Mother's funeral and all the people that came had gone home and left just me and Dad in the house. I don't know how I could tell that, but I could. Dad said him and me had to have a glass of sherry together because of the occasion, only I don't remember ever drinking sherry in my life and I'm pretty sure Dad didn't either. It came to me that Dad was a bit squiffy, which he never was, but it seemed to be all right for him to be squiffy in the dream. He spoke very civil and merry to me and didn't even raise his voice. 'We must take comfort in the Lord, Vera,' he said to me. We were sat on either side of the fire in the front room, which is wrong, too, because Dad would never let a fire be lit as early as October when Mother went. 'Think of the life of our Lord, Vera,' he says, 'and take comfort.' And it somehow seemed I was little again and ever so much smaller than Dad, which is silly because I was thirty-two at Mother's funeral. 'At Advent, He came down and was born a little baby amongst us,' he says, 'as a sign and a mystery to us all. And on Good Friday, He was crucified on our joint behalf. On the Third Day He rose again. And on the Queen's Official Birthday, He ascended into heaven.' I must say he said it all in a very comforting way, and I had a warm glow inside. Or perhaps that was the sherry. But the last bit didn't sound quite right and he stopped speaking and rubbed his chin for a long time, seemingly thinking about it. Then the answer come to him and he looked over at me and gave me this lovely smile.

'Firework night isn't in it,' he says to me. And then I woke up.

I have been thinking about that dream all day. It has been on my mind so much that I clean forgot about all our present trials. They only come back to my mind when I started to say to you about it just now. I think maybe there is a lesson for all of us in that. I think maybe Dad was trying to tell me something like that in the dream, even if the dream was all mixed up. I think he was maybe saying for us all to have a new heart and take up hope for the future. With the way Tim and Madeline have been left, that might be a tall order, but you never can tell how long a thing like that will be permanent, can you? Maybe even tomorrow or the day after, things will take a turn for the up and up. You never know about things like that. I do hope and pray for Tim and Madeline's sake it will take a turn like that. It would be so nice to be able to say to them about how everything is after all turning out for the best. It would be no more than they deserved to know they weren't after all going into liquidization, which is Tim's greatest fear nowadays. 'Our ship has come home,' I would say to them, 'our ship has come home at last and all our troubles are over. Our ship has come home and Lloyds will ring the Libertine Bell.'

WHEN THE SAILOR WAS FAR AWAY

For Faith Bowman Davey

Ahoy there! The ship's sinking!

The service in here. Look at her, look, down the other end there. Counting her fingernails. Must be in love, you reckon? Time was when you could get a bit of service down this end. This used to be the posh end. You know, the Saloon, higher prices, no working clothes, separate barmaid all its own. Before they knocked the whole thing into the one. Here she comes now. Taking her time.

I missed you, darling, where you been? Where were you when the sailor was far away? Usual, darling, now when do I ever drink anything different? Ah, where were you forty years ago when I was looking for you?

Forty years? What am I bleeding talking about, mate? Sixty if it's an inch. Been cracking the same jokes too long, mate. You get that way at my age. Pay no attention. It don't bother me none. Mud in your eye.

I don't think she really appreciated the joke, mate, do you? Youngsters. Think anyone more than twice their age must be dead from the neck up. Don't pay you no proper heed. Don't see you properly because they only half look and don't hear you properly because they only half listen. Still, you and me was the same at their age, eh, mate? That's the difference, isn't it? The difference with being old and looking back. We've *been* young but they've never *been* old. We can remember what young's like but they can only guess what old's like. And remembering's a lot less bother than guessing, eh? Remembering's second nature at our age, mate. Well, at *my* age, begging your pardon. Reckon I could give you, what, forty years? You're only a boy, mate. Born with the century, that's

79

me. Anyway, perhaps she's foreign. That would explain it. You get a lot of foreign behind the bar these days. I been round the world, mate, and I'll tell you this. The hardest thing of all to hear in a foreign tongue is a joke. Yes. Got to make allowances.

I was at sea in two world wars, you know. Royal Navy in the first, merchant service in the second. That teaches you to take a joke all right. The sea, not world wars. They tell you if you can't take a joke, you should never have joined the Andrew, and they're dead bleeding right. Out of sight of dry land, a man that can't take a joke will end up doing murder or doing himself in.

When I was a kid, when I left the old Board School at going on fourteen, there was nothing round here, mate, nothing at all. Slightest bleeding hint of a job and a queue formed in a minute. Grown men with growing families fighting each other to get a day's work on the docks. Fighting each other to get even a bleeding boy's job, most days. My old man and three of the four brothers, they was all of them lightermen and in pretty steady work, so we never exactly starved, but even they couldn't get me took on. Or perhaps they wasn't trying too hard if they had to look in the faces of their mates and neighbours what needed the wages far worse than we did, hungry women and children looking out of them men's eyes. Wouldn't blame them now if they did tell me a white lie or two to give a start to a desperate man, mate, wouldn't blame them a bit. But back then weren't now, of course. A normal young chap wants to be up and doing, wants to be a part and parcel of things, wants to make a man of himself. And if you didn't know someone back then to get you a start, there wasn't much a young chap could be up and doing *at*, apart from thieving and fighting. Not that I was much of a one for that, not the thieving, anyway. Ma brought us up very respectable. If any of us had been took thieving, I think she'd have hanged us personal, grown men or not. Only a little slip of a thing, but she run that house like a Tartar. Anyway, weren't but only the one thing I ever wanted to be part and parcel *of*. The water, mate, the river. All our family was watermen. Even Ma's father used to sail a Thames barge, though he was a cripple old grandad laid up with his legs by the time I'm talking about.

London's been robbed, mate, robbed of her ships. On a good day I still walk along to Tower Bridge and do you know what always hits me? It ain't the lorries along the old Highway and it ain't the millionaire playboats in St Katharine's Dock. That's all right by me, mate. Nothing wrong with that. No. It's the Pool. I just can't seem to get used to the Pool of London being so bleeding empty. Nothing in it but HMS *Belfast* at the pontoon and a few diesel tripper-boats going by. When I was a boy you had a job to see the water in the Pool of London. On a busy day, a clever chap who knew what he was about could walk from Custom House Quay to Hay's Wharf with dry boots and never touch a bridge to win a two-bob bet. Done it myself. Quay to lighter to barge to lighter and so forth. Had to know what you was about, mind, and not get underfoot. Them old watermen had a job of work to do, and no easy job at that. They didn't have no smiles of welcome for any young clever Dick what got in their way. A real man's job. Like trying to do navvy work standing on the end of a slow see-saw worked by a drunkard, our Jack used to say. But there was skill there as well as sweat, mate, something you could take a pride in. I used to love to watch it, the whole Pool swarming with men doing men's work. Half Wapping was at work on the Pool on a busy day. That's what I wanted to be a part and parcel of, mate. Funny when you think of it. Most of today's kids, even with all this stuff about unemployment, they wouldn't even look at a job like that. Stay on the Giro for life before they'd even have a try at a job where you come home dog-tired every night and the first slip you make's likely to be the last. We didn't have no Giro, did we?

The only real work I did get, apart from penny-halfpenny errand jobs, wasn't really a proper job at all, if that don't sound too Irish. The work was real enough, but it was almost a charity thing, really. Lord Thing used to run it; his name's gone, but he weren't a proper lord, just a titled grocer, and very big in the Quakers. He run a scheme where lads was took off the streets of the East End and put to do healthy useful work on the land. Lord Thing's land, in Kent. At a wage a sight less than a grown man's, of course, but I wasn't thinking too much about that at my age. Funny enough, Ma were against it because she didn't want us taking no charity, did she? And she thought the lads on a scheme like that would be dead rough. Old man talked her round, though, said it would build me up. Fresh country air and that. And there was her married sister in Maidstone what Ma seemed to think could somehow keep her baby boy safe from the entire county of Kent. Well, she was dead wrong there because I never did get as far as Maidstone and to this day I ain't got the first idea what Auntie Lil looked like. Ma never had a photo of her in the house, and they never come calling. Maidstone was a long way for ordinary working people in them days. Railway tickets and days off was all very well for bankers' clerks and publicans, but the ordinary working chap with a family couldn't run to it. Never expected to, what's more.

On the first evening after work, some of us young chaps got to chatting. Getting to know each other, like. And there was this young ginger chap from Plaistow way called Percy Danger. That's a name you never see a boy called now, Percy. Why do some names come and go? Never worked it out. Anyway, Percy says he'd fight any one of us for the sport of it, and a shilling stakes too if we wanted. He weren't a big lad, but he had that wiry build and he had the look in his eye, mate. Only four of us took him up, me included. Bare-knuckle fighting, not Queensberry rules, but fair enough fights. The word got round somehow and a regular little crowd of blokes gathered round us in the field to watch. Women too, rough enough to prove old Ma right at a glance. Well, Percy polished off the first three in short order. He was game as you like and he could dig a bit for a little 'un, but it was his hands as beat them, mate. Never seen hands as quick, clip you before you could blink. But I was watching him, and I could see he was very easy provoked. Bertie Ross was the second one he fought and straight off Bertie bangs him one on the nose. Percy went bleeding berserk, mate. Bertie was so surprised he was down and out before he could spot how Percy was leaving himself wide open around the breadbasket. Bertie Ross never was too quick on the uptake, but I spotted it all right. Come my turn, I kept covered up as best I could and tried for his nose, but he'd had enough of that from Bertie. So I gets in as close as I can and tells him a few home truths what I just made up about red-headed little so-and-so's from Plaistow and that done the trick. Nearly done me and all, mate, because even out of control he still clipped me four or five times about the head before I could give him the big one, notwithstanding I was already set up and cocked for it. Quick hands, mate, never seen the like. But I got him, though. Flat-footed, with all my weight behind it. 'Oof!' he says, and sits down smartish. Never seen a bloke look more surprised. Not in no hurry to get up again, neither. Never even looked like beating the count.

That was Sailor Danger I beat there, mate. Champion of the Home Fleet. Fought professional before crowned heads in the Albert Hall. Much later, of course, after the war. Best man never to win the British welterweight championship, mate.

On the night I beat him, he didn't hold no grudge at all. Straight up to me as soon as he gets his breath back and shakes me by the hand. 'Good for you, you foxy basket!' he says, 'Next time I does *you*.' Never was no next time, though. Percy Danger and me was best mates from then on, best mates.

After two or three months, me and Percy had both of us
had quite enough of healthy useful work on the land, so we
went on the tramp. Percy were dead set against going back to
London. I had a kind of feeling that he'd been threw out by
his old man anyway, but you couldn't ask Percy Danger
about a thing like that. He were that hot-tempered. 'Bugger
the Smoke,' says Percy after we camped out the first night, 'I'll
join the Navy. See the world. Sail round the Cape of Good
Horn. You game?' I'd never even thought about it till then,
but I were that surprised I said 'Yes' straight off. So we legged
it to Chatham. Two days walking, it took us. And when we
got there, guess what? Another bleeding queue, mate, a
bleeding great line of blokes ahead of us waiting to sign on.
Nearly turned on my heel and walked off in disgust, but
Percy said not to waste a long walk and why not wait our
turn? So we waited and they give us the medical and such
and we told some barefaced lies about when we was born and
they signed us on. Both of us. For six years.

And then someone told us that war had been declared two
days previous. That's right, mate, first thing either of us knew
about it. No telly then, nor no wireless. And I hadn't seen a
paper in a week, and I don't think Percy could read that good
at the best of times. And the news we did see or hear, well,
how much interest is a normal young chap of that age going
to take in politics and foreign affairs and such? I often
wondered over the years whether Percy and me would have
still joined up if we'd known beforehand about the war. I
reckon we would still have signed on, even though I felt sort
of diddled at the time. Percy would for sure, raring to get at
the enemy as soon as he heard, Percy was. Straight off
making a song and dance about getting on a fighting ship and
doing his bit and that. 'You'll do your bit all right, son,' says
the Chiefy, 'but you better get used to the idea that you'll do
it wherever the sodding Andrew sends you.' He were right
and all. Percy Danger and me never even put to sea on the

same ship, mate. In fact, I don't even know for sure if Percy ever put to sea at all. Separated us, they did. I have no idea to this day what sort of war Percy Danger had. Me? Crossed the Atlantic thirteen times doing escort duty, and never once saw a ship's gun fired in anger. Heard them all right, but never saw them. You don't see much sea stoking boilers. Stoker, right through the war.

Look out, she's back. You been away so long I forgot how beautiful you were, darling. Just the bottle this time, freshen it up. Cheer up, it ain't the end of the world. That's tomorrow week.

A brother is a funny thing, mate. I had the four of them to start with, but three was killed in the first war. Jack was killed at Ypres and Harold at Vimy Ridge. And Sam was killed by a fourth-storey chimney-pot come down in a gale in Tooley Street. They was the three that was watermen in peacetime. A good lot older than me and sort of heroes when I was a kid. The fighting Cobhams, they called them. Cocks of the walk down Wapping Wall, though they wouldn't none of them cross Ma. All of them gone. And what was left me? Bleeding Wilf. Bleeding pansy Jesus-loves-you Wilfred. Ma's pet, teacher's pet, starched-collar Sunday School milksop Wilfred. Two and a half years older than me, but I can't remember a time when I couldn't have thrashed him one-handed. *Look after your brother, boys. He's too delicate to look after himself.* He were too bleeding fly to need to, mate, take my word for it. He knew he had the rest of us beat hollow just by being so good and holy and weak we couldn't none of us lay a finger on him. He was too good and holy to say so, but when you looked him in his holy bleeding eye you *knew*, and he let you know he knew that you knew. Weak? That turned out the biggest laugh of all, mate. His poor weak heart what kept him out of uniform through two world wars, it never did let him down. Stroke got him in the end. Seventy-eight, and still as active as ever. Fell down in Fine Fare and dead when the ambulance came. Weak be buggered. There were times as a kid when I hated Wilf, and more than once in mid-Atlantic half-blind with sweat and dust I thought of him at home all safe and snug and what I thought is better left unsaid. But if I'd known then he'd still be hopping around like a good 'un at seventy-eight, I don't know what I mightn't have done, and that's the truth, mate. Still, Wilfred it was, the only brother left me after the war. And like I say, a brother is a funny thing.

When I come back on my first shore leave at the end of the war, you could have knocked me down with a feather when I seen what Wilf had done. I hadn't been home in a year and I feared the worst, mate. Wilf had wrote me that Ma was very broke up over the boys getting killed, and the old man couldn't do heavy work no more with his back. Wilf had his clerking job in the insurance, but he wasn't hardly earning no more than a boy, and I weren't in no position myself to send all that much home. It was a worrying thing to think about. But when I got there, Wilf had worked the oracle. Ma was never the same woman again after she lost her boys, but Wilf was always her favourite and he was a great comfort to her. She told me once in private she would have made away with herself when Sam died but for Wilfred. And the old man was wore out with years of heavy work and hard times, but Wilf had still managed to set them up so they was never better off in their whole lives, not for money anyway.

What Wilf had done was this, mate. He had the two of them fixed up in a nice little fish-and-chip business in the Whitechapel Road. Near the London Hospital, just along from Mile End Gate. How he managed that I never did find out. Whenever I asked him about it, he just tapped the side of his nose and looked holy. 'The Lord provides,' he says.

Neat little place, it was, with living quarters in five rooms above the shop. Mansionette, they'd call it now, because it had its own street door without having to come through the shop. Enough room to take in lodgers, except they never needed no lodger money because the shop was such a going concern. Turns out Ma and Pa are natural-born businessmen, which is as much of a surprise as our Wilf being a fixer. Ma was always ferocious house-proud and that shop was spotless, and even with no schooling worth mentioning she never had no trouble at all counting money. And the old man had got to know a drinking chap or two in Billingsgate over the years, which didn't go to waste when it come time to buy fish, did it? What with Wilf doing the books and helping out in the shop on busy nights, they were doing all right, mate. So when I first come home and seen it all, it was a real load off my mind. 'I have got to hand it to you,' I says to Wilfred, 'you have done a real man's job there. I don't mind admitting I never thought you had it in you, and I don't mind admitting I was wrong, neither.' 'The Lord provides,' says Wilf, only he couldn't seem to get the proper look in his eyes to go along with his holy face.

I used to look forward to that shop when I was at sea. It was a real lively place, always something happening. The customers used to come just to see what Pa would get up to next; he was always one for a laugh and a joke even when times was at their worst. 'Are you sure you wants this here cod?' he'd ask them, 'Are you very very sure you wants it? It's that fresh I ain't sure it's dead yet.' And the characters you used to get going in there. There was these two Jewish brothers run a second-hand clothes stall over the road; they was always in there. They had this act they used to do with Pa, making out they was simple and just off the boat speaking bad English and Pa making out he's trying to get rid of them. Real old hams, the lot of them. The other customers used to love it. 'Put me please one quarter chopped and fried,' says Number One Brother. 'Don't sell it,' says Pa. 'Put me please two portions lox,' says Number Two Brother. 'What's lox?' says Pa. 'Hah,' says Number Two, 'lox is smoked solomon.' 'Oy,' says Number One, 'you know how much is smoked solomon?

We shall go bang corrupt.' 'No call for it,' Pa says. 'I take please one dozen goldfishes,' says Number One Brother. 'Don't do them,' says Pa. 'What kind fish shop this is you don't got no fishes?' says Number One. 'You don't got no fishes, you will go bang corrupt, I swear you,' Number Two says. Customers all in stitches, Ma and Pa could have charged admission.

In three years that little business done so well that they was able to buy the place outright with Wilf going equal shares. Ma and Pa never owned any other place nor their parents before them, so they was a bit chary about taking it on, but Wilf made them do it. Wilf was the brains behind it all, of course, and he could always win Ma round to his side. And Pa was of an age by then when he had more sense than start a row he couldn't win, mate. In his heart of hearts, Pa never really took to Wilf the same as he did the rest of us, but a man what gets to a certain age can stomach an awful lot for the sake of a bit of peace and quiet. Wilf didn't get no argument from Pa.

Different with me, of course. I weren't no wise old man, mate, I was still Jack the bleeding lad. I appreciated what Wilf was doing, and I looked on that shop as my real home from home, but I weren't about to let his holy highness tell me how to do my own business, nor his toffee-nosed wife. Married the year after the war. Clarice, her name was, and she hated me on sight. Her mother was cook-housekeeper to some nob family up West, and Clarice thought she was a touch too good for the Cobhams. Living above a chippie was bad enough, but having a father- and brother-in-law what both *drank* – well, she found that hard to swallow, mate. Wilf was still very hot on the Chapel business the whole time, see, and the temperance. That was how he'd got to meet her. And he would preach to me about it, see? I think it was her egged him on to it in private due to she had it in for me, because Pa never had no trouble from Wilf on that score. Or perhaps Wilf had just decided that Pa was beyond help by then. Anyway, I wouldn't have none of it, of course. You know what sailors are, as they say. I told Wilf that I more than pulled my weight with money and with helping out in the shop for no wages when I was staying there, but my life was my own. And if him and his snob wife didn't like it they could stick it in their pipe and smoke it, if they was man enough to have a smoke.

And here she is at last! Full light-and-bitter this time, sweetheart, and a pound out the till. Bet you ain't no snob, eh? Know what it means, 'snob'? When we was kids, Pa used to do all the family cobbling of an evening. Repair work, soles and heels and iron tacks for our boots. Got his own last, the lot. 'I am my own snob,' he used to tell us, 'I does all my own snobbing. I ain't proud.' Snobs? Cobblers.

They say putting it in your pipe and smoking it is bad for you anyway nowadays. Never done me no harm, mate. They say everything's bad for you nowadays if you believe half what you read. Well, I say every minute you live takes another sixty seconds off your life. Wilf went very strong on that health-food stuff towards the end, you know. I broke my last good tooth eating wholemeal bread in Wilf's kitchen. I reckon you can't afford to go worrying about that sort of thing the whole time. I reckon all this medical stuff on telly and in the papers and that does as much harm as good, mate. Who'd ever catch these new-fangled diseases if they didn't read about them in the paper?

I reckon it was Wilf's Clarice kept me at sea, you know. Left to himself, I reckon Wilf might have left me alone to live my own life, and if he'd done that I might have stayed ashore for good when I come out the Andrew in 1920. I certainly never wanted to see another bleeding boiler-room, mate, and that's a fact. But Clarice wouldn't let him alone so he couldn't let me alone, could he? We had the mother and father of all rows over it, me and Wilf, and me not ashore three weeks. I didn't have no time to get fixed up with any dry-land work apart from the shop, and there was no way I could stay in the same place as Wilf after that row, mate. It was worse for knowing I couldn't lay a finger on him, and worse still seeing that Ma and Pa didn't really need me at all with Wilf around. I had to get out. And the only way out for a man with my record was to go back to sea. So that's just what I done, but as a deckie; no more stoking for me. And do you know what? I was at sea for the next twenty years, and in all that twenty years I never spoke to brother Wilfred but twice, and that was at the two funerals. Ma's and Pa's, within a twelvemonth in '34. A brother is a funny thing, and no mistake.

I say at sea, mate, but half the time I was hardly out of sight of land. Coasters. Colliers. Irish and Continental ferries, that class of thing. I'd lost any notion of being away from home for weeks and months at a stretch, especially after I got married myself and had a proper home of my own to come back to. Do you know, I still live in the same place, mate? The same flat from 1924 right up to today. They wanted to move me out into one of them council homes when the missus died ten year ago but I wouldn't have it. Them flats means something to me. I saved them flats, didn't I? When they wanted to pull them down that time. Everyone else in the block would've taken the persuasion money, but I wouldn't budge and it were 100 per cent or nothing, see? In the local paper, it was. Secure tenants, see, controlled rent. Couldn't get me out legal if I didn't want to go, so they dropped the whole scheme. Now there's talk of making the place one of them what-do-you-callits, listed buildings, and then nobody can touch it. Suits me. I am content to die in that flat, mate. They can do what they like after I'm gone.

No, mate, I went round the world below decks in the Navy and the world is the most boring place on earth to go round that way. Take it from me, mate. The short trips was always the ones for me after that. You get every bit as much variety and that as you want in that, even on the ferry-boats, where you'd think it would be just back-and-forth, back-and-forth, yawning dull. I was on the Liverpool–Douglas run for nine months back, oh, before I got wed, and I was never in my life at sea with such a crew of wild men. Even the officers was less than 20 shilling in the pound. Skipper thought he were sailing a regular Cunarder, I swear he did. Floated around in a cloud of gin fumes, talking to titled passengers that wasn't there. Been mined in the war, they said, never got over it proper. He used to tell you the same jokes time and time again, and the same stories. Got on your nerves. 'In the submarine service, Potter,' he'd say, and he always called you Potter whoever you was, 'in the submarine service, the real danger is not the enemy. The enemy is not seen from one week to the next, Potter. The true dangers are confinement and boredom. The slightest thing can send a man running amok in such circumstances, Potter.' Yes, I can just hear him. 'The secret is to keep the minds of the crew occupied. Plenty of spit and polish. Competitions between watches with the results pinned up on the board. Recreational activities, chess, ludo, cards, especially cards,' and he'd put on that special little face to tell you the joke was coming, 'yes, Potter. A lot of bridge under the water.' And he'd lift himself up and down on the balls of his feet waiting for you to laugh. You had to laugh polite, like, because if you didn't laugh, he'd cry. Quietly, without making no noise. Beamish, his name was. We was all under strict orders to laugh at his jokes, no matter how many times we already heard them. You mightn't believe it, but I once seen the same man barehanded stop a fight between two roaring drunk Irish firemen trying to split each other with iron shovels. Nobody else would go within ten yards of it, but Beamish just floats up to them casual, not even trying to dodge, and stands there stroking his chin. A little stocky chap, he were. 'Potter,' he says, 'stop that at *once*.' And they did. Yes. He never seemed to make any mistakes in the actual sailing of the ship, either. He were never sober, but the only time you ever seen him take a drink, you had to be at the helm when we was coming into Douglas harbour. When the quay was properly in sight, he'd take out a hip-flask. 'Midships,' he'd say (or whatever), and then have a long pull at the flask. 'Potter,' he'd say, wiping his joke-coming face, 'this Man is an island.'

I'm the last of our line, you know. Last of the fighting Cobhams. We never had no kids, me and Greta, no more did Wilf and Clarice. Always been a source of regret to me. To Greta, too, though she never said a word of complaint. Not her way. Make a joke out of it, she would. 'No children have blessed our marriage,' she used to say, 'and no children is a blessing many another marriage I knows could well do with.' But she felt it all right, I could always tell. And even if you do believe in miracles, mate, it's too late now for me. The old name dies with me, mate.

Clarice was killed in the Blitz. Still quite a young woman. Direct hit. On a public convenience, of all places, in Old Ford. Raid caught Clarice out in the open and they reckoned she panicked and dived into the first open door she come to. It was the gents' side, see, so she must have been in a bit of a panic. Clarice was far too prim and proper to make that sort of mistake unless she was in a bit of a panic. It near broke Wilf, you know. Her being gone, I mean, not her being round the gent's side. She was the only one in there anyway, as far as they could tell. But Wilf was like a little old man for the rest of his life, and him only forty-three and all. Still, he saw most of them off in the finish, what?

Wilf and me made up at Clarice's funeral. I had a hell of a job to get compassionate for that, but you got to do it for a brother, ain't you, even if you've hardly spoke to him for twenty years. I say made up, but it was more like we just carried on like there'd never been no break. I said to him why don't he move in with me and Greta, rattling about like a pea in a barrel in that bleeding great place over the shop. Very independent though, Wilf. Wouldn't hear of it. Very polite and grateful, like, but wouldn't hear of it. He stayed on his own in that place till the day he died, you know. Very like me in that much, at any rate, liked his own old home.

'The trouble with experience, Potter,' mad Beamish used to say to you, 'the trouble with experience is it's incurable.' Old Beamish didn't half get on your nerves, mate, but he managed to talk a lot of sense too, sometimes. It takes a lifetime to know what I knows now, but when you really needs to know it is before you've learnt it, while you're still young. I don't really need to know most of it now, mate. I don't really need to *do* much any more. Good job too, because there's lots I can't do any more supposing I was to try. You get like that. You never have no trouble remembering it, neither. The old body will soon tell you if you try to do something it don't like. See this here? This ain't my own hip, mate. Plastic. Ten years and more since I had my own hip joints. Still, thousands worse off than that.

But I did find it a bit much getting up to see Wilf with the hips. Been a walker all my life, me. Never had no time for buses and cabs and that, not that I could ever afford cabs after I retired. The old pension's nothing, is it? I'd a bit put by, of course, but not long after I finished was the Monopoly money time with the prices going up and up. Wilf had a bit more than me put by, what with selling the shop as a lock-up business and having a few policies from his time in the insurance office what he'd always kept up the payments on. But even Wilfred felt the pinch towards the end. So where we used to spend some time in each others' company nearly every day, it got that I couldn't manage it more than once a week with the old pins.

That's what I miss most, you know. Them weekly chats that me and Wilf used to have right up to the end. All the other things I used to miss, I've had the time to get over it, but I ain't got over Wilf going yet and I don't expect to be given time enough to get over it neither. Still, you can't go brooding, can you? Better to remember the good times and forget the bad. Them chats I used to have with Wilf is rum things to look back on, mind. He got a bit odd towards the end, old Wilf. His eyes was too bad for him to read his watch, you know. The only way he could tell if it was time to get up was to go to the window and see if the Midland Bank was open. If the bank door was shut, he went back to bed. One Whit Monday he went back to bed eight times before I come round at two in the afternoon.

I say chats, but they was really more like rows, you know. What it was, me and Wilf had got to an age where we didn't really need to say nothing to each other no more. I don't think we realized it ourselves at the time, but all we really had to tell each other every week was we ain't dead yet. Anything else we'd already said a hundred times. For myself, I might have been happy just to sit in each other's company and say nothing, but Wilf never could just sit quiet and like I say, he got a bit odd towards the end. So we used to sit and have this good old row, mate. Yes. Know what we used to row about? Bridges. We used to have the same bleeding argument every week about the exact order of the bridges over the Thames. Clarice was always a one for the pleasure-boats, see, and Wilf kept up the habit in her memory. That was the nearest Wilfred Cobham ever come to following the family trade, a pleasure-boat up to Kew or Hampton Court. He used to make out he was the number one expert on London bridges, and I used to rib him about it, and it just sort of grew into this regular half-serious row every week. It weren't a *real* row, of course. More like a game to pass the time; you can see that looking back on it. We weren't really saying anything to each other; all we was telling each other was we ain't dead yet. 'London Bridge, now, that's the next after Tower, and then you got Southwark, lot of people miss that one – ' 'Wake up, you dozy old basket, you missed the Cannon Street railway bridge, railway bridges is bridges too, ain't they?' 'Who says so? Who says so?' *We're still here, my old mate. He ain't got round to us yet.* '. . . then you has Chiswick Bridge, Chiswick, that's the lowest bridge on the navigable Thames, that is. And then the Barnes railway, Kew railway, Kew proper, Twickenham, Richmond railway, Richmond – 'Hang about, hang about, what about the footbridge at Richmond Lock? You always miss that one, expert be buggered . . .' *We ain't dead yet, brother, we ain't dead yet.*

Did I tell you I got to see old Percy Danger again? Good old Sailor Danger, best man never to win the British welterweight title. I never actually seen him fight professional myself, but I seen his picture in the papers and the boxing mags often enough, and a right rough-looking little basket he grew up into and all. But he dropped out of the news well before I was more or less settled down myself, and I couldn't see no way to get in touch with him by then. Never looked to meet him again, but I did. After a gap of more than forty years, mate. At the boxing.

That was another rum thing about old Wilfred. He got to know all sorts of people in all sorts of lines of business over the years, and if he'd been a more ambitious sort of a chap I reckon he could have died rich. You'd be surprised what old Wilf could fix for you, mate, you really would. But he had no real go in him after Clarice went; the rest of his life he was just going through the motions. Even with all that old church stuff he always kept up with, even that was just going through the motions. And maybe a lot of the people he might be doing this little bit of business or that with, you might say they was a bit, well, dodgy, and Clarice would have given him merry hell for mixing with the likes of that, but Wilf never actually *done* nothing Clarice wouldn't have let him, never done it *himself*. Very strict about that, he were. Which is why he never would go to the fights. He could always get you a ticket or two, but he never come with you himself. I always had to go without him.

I'm talking about the best part of twenty year ago, of course, when I could still get about like a good 'un. ABA Finals, it were. Don't remember nothing about the fights, so they can't have been much cop, but I'll never forget the surprise I got when I saw old Percy Danger sitting there in the bar. No mistaking that face. Same rough-looking little basket I used to see in the boxing mags forty years earlier. The forty years showed all right; it were a real old outdoor face, an old-fashioned seaman's face. Weatherbeaten, some might call it, but that face had beaten the weather, mate. Hands down. Sailor Danger! Sitting in a wheelchair.

He didn't see me at first, so I walks up and says, 'Well then, Percy,' and then I bent down and told him them home truths I made up all them years ago about little ginger so-and-so from Plaistow. 'I knows *you*,' he says, 'you are Albert bleeding Cobham, and next time I does *you*.' Remembered me straight off. I sat down and had a drink with him and a good old chat. And I'll say one thing for him. You know how an old boy can't seem to leave out bragging about all the fights he won when he was a kid? Percy never done that, not once, and he had a lot more to brag about than most. Not that keen on talking about the navy days, neither. 'Thought I was going to see the world, didn't I?' he says, 'See the dusky maidens of the South Sea Islands and the Boris dancers of Vladivostok. Well, I seen Invergordon, and it's the Alaska of the north, that place. The Alaska of the bleeding north.' Turns out his face got the old weather job selling the evening paper for thirty year at a stand in Tooting Broadway. Been in the wheelchair thirty year, some unpronounceable doctor stuff wrong with his back.

Well, one drink led to another, and I'll tell you what, mate. I don't know if old Percy ever did have any sort of a head for drink, but he'd lost it by then if he did. Couldn't bleeding shut him up after he'd had a couple. All at the top of his voice, too. He weren't none too polite, neither. 'Scrapes and bones,

Albert,' he says, 'you and me was brung up on scrapes and bones, but we had the guts to make a man of ourself. This lot today are bleeding rubbish with their Yankee music and Eurovision Declaration of Human Rights. I wouldn't give you a penny bleeding piece for any of them fights tonight.' And he went on and on about it, glaring round the room the way a bullying chap will do to catch the eye of someone to have a row with. There was lots of young chaps there, of course, but they was either ignoring him or making out it was all a big joke. That only seemed to make Percy worse, though, and in the finish the steward chap come round the bar and more or less told me to get Percy out of there. He were quite a polite young chap and you could see his point, unless you was Percy Danger. 'What's he saying?' says Percy, 'Speak up, damn you! My ears ain't getting no younger. Come a bit closer,' and the young chap bends over to speak to him. And Percy clips him with the sweetest right hook anyone's seen all night, and the young chap goes down like a sack of spuds. I know wheelchair people get to have strong arms and that from pushing theirself around, but that was still something to see, mate. Sailor Danger, sixty-five years old and sat in a wheelchair, still putting his man away with just the one punch. The young chap didn't press charges, of course. No young chap wants to put it around that he's been knocked cold by an old drunk cripple of sixty-five sat in a wheelchair.

Never tried to keep in touch with Percy after that, of course. Who'd want to keep in touch with a cantankerous trouble-making old basket like that?

The year Wilf died, it were that year we had the very hot summer, with the water rations. Nineteen seventy-six, would it be? Too bleeding hot to do a thing, weren't it? I don't know how anything ever gets done in hot countries where it's like that all the time. I suppose they're born and bred to it, but I could never be doing with it, mate. Never in a hundred years. After the funeral, I didn't go out of doors for weeks. Too hot to move, too hot to think. Neighbours was very good about it. Come round to see was I all right and bring a bit of shopping and that. Not a lot you need at my age, anyway. I hardly noticed the days going by, to tell you the truth. An old man don't, you know. But even that summer did finally break, and I was soon feeling a bit better in myself and I started to get out and about again. And do you know what, mate? There was a complete new house built where I could only remember bare ground. Bomb site the council cleared and levelled a few years back and a ship's chandler's before it were a bomb site, that was all I remembered, and now there was this complete new two-storey house with curtains up and the lawn turfed. Seemed like it sprung up overnight. Set me thinking of when I was a kid of, oh, six or seven and there was building work going on down the end of our road. We used to play on that site, us kids, when we could dodge the watchman and keep it secret from our ma. It was a special place, almost a secret kids' place away from the grown-ups, I don't know quite how to put it. But the point is it was a *permanent* place, that site, it was for ever. None of us kids ever doubted that. That's the way it goes, mate. When you're a little kid, it takes for ever to build a house, and when you're old they bleeding spring up overnight. Old Father Time keeps rolling along.

At last, at last, she's come back to join us. Nothing for me, darling. I've had my ration. But where were you, darling? Where were you forty years ago when I was looking for you? Where were you when the sailor was far away?

A FORMER SECURITY WITH
HELEN DAMNATION

For Valerie Lilley

You see, the thing is, in my heart of hearts I always knew that Willy was going to last for ever, or for as much of it as pleased him. Everybody who knew him any length of time must have felt something like that. He was always so maddeningly bloody indomitable, so irrepressible, so *indestructible*.

First time I met him, or saw him really, you couldn't properly call it a meeting, he was already by way of being a minor celebrity, though I'd never heard of him. Are you old enough to remember the Light Programme? Pirate Radio? When Covent Garden was strictly Grand Opera, Magistrates' Court and Wholesale Vegetables? You could get a drink almost round the clock in Covent Garden, but you couldn't have found a hand-crafted marionette to save your life, not for cash money, and anyone in studs and an OTT orange Mohican would have got pelted with broken fruit and lethal verbals by nasty rough men in working-dirty overalls.

That was where I first saw him, in a room above a saloon bar in Covent Garden. We'd nipped up from a pub-crawl along Fleet Street and the Strand in the hope of beating Last Orders by spending some time and money to get ourselves accepted in one of the market houses. Five or six of us, all in our first or second year at King's, all fresh up from Bradford or Bangor or Bodmin or Banff, all prepared to walk a mile in the wrong direction rather than open a map or ask our way and let ourselves be seen as strangers in town. Do you know, I can't remember the exact year for sure? But it was the early sixties, the start of the folk-music boom.

It's still a bit of a mystery to me how we managed to graduate from the saloon bar to the upstairs place where the club was. All I remember is somehow being there. It was typical of that kind of place, dim, lighted candles in wine bottles, performer on a high stool at one end, audience on low chairs or standing at the back, attentive, all ages from teens to fifties, quite a few beards, lumberjack shirts and collars and ties in about equal numbers, lots of CND badges (the first time round, of course). I expect if I went back now I'd find it scruffy, stuffy, smoky and thoroughly uncomfortable, but at the time the atmosphere seemed terrific. The beer must have helped, but Willy helped even more. There was a big genial drunken middle-aged bearded American lurching around at the back in an off-white stetson, beaming at everyone and scratching himself. Later on he lay down behind the piano and went to sleep, and someone told us proudly that he was *the* (Inaudible) Adams in a tone of voice that showed you got Brownie points for having *the* Inaudible Adams passed out pissed behind your piano. But when we arrived, Inaudible Adams was still going strong. He was engaged in some fairly good-natured heckling made up of cracks not even he could have called wise mixed in with loud, genuine and brilliantly timed farts. He really was quite funny, to anyone who hadn't yet seen quite enough amusing drunks, thank you. Willy handled him beautifully, capping every line, getting the audience to give Inaudible a standing ovation, telling him he wouldn't be lonely if he went and leant on the wall of the gents because that was plastered too, all standard stuff as old as the original stand-up comic, but it was the *delivery* that got to you. He was fairly ordinary to look at, Willy, young guy about twenty with black hair in a semicrew, but he had real presence all the same. You couldn't see how he managed it, but every eye in the place stayed on him unless he decided otherwise. He had a fairish singing tenor and a strong high speaking voice with that dry Glasgow manner that a bit later on helped make Billy Connolly his first million. 'Och, noo, hoots, Hamish!' says Inaudible Adams, 'Wull yee no sing us a

Jacobite song?' '?' says Willy, '?' – this great wide innocent look on his face – 'oh, a *Jacobite* song. Listen, I'd love to oblige, but there are no Jacobite songs,' and now it's Inaudible's turn to say, '?' 'No, really,' says Willy, 'there are *none*. Oh, I expect you've just got yourself the new Topic album by Peggy Seeger and Ewan Whose Army, but those aren't Jacobite songs. Those were all written seventy, eighty, ninety years after the event by middle-aged middle-class maiden ladies in Edinburgh New Town sitting-rooms, enamoured of the Wild Romantic Gael from reading too many Waverley novels. One, since you ask, is too many Waverley novels. Whereas your actual Wild Romantic Gael was lying out on the hill after Culloden getting his Wild Romantic Arse frozen off, and if he came down off the hill he got his Wild Romantic Arse shot off by Butcher Cumberland and his merry men and that was when they were in a *good* mood. That man was in the original No Win situation. No Arse situation. That man was most definitely not thinking or singing "Wae's me for Prince Cherlie". No. That man was thinking, *FUCK THIS SHITE!* In Wild Romantic Gaelic.' Collapse of Inaudible Adams.

And I thought, *I know what I want to be when I grow up. I want to be that guy there on the stool.* The others seemed to feel the same. When we found out from the guy taking the money at the table by the door that Willy had a residency at the club every Tuesday, we became instant regulars.

After a few weeks, we'd done such a good job of spreading the word at college that you had to come really early to have any chance of getting a seat, and probably more than half the audience was students. Willy, being the great sharpie he was, cottoned on to this straight away and started playing to the student gallery, or student first four rows in this case, half the time seemingly buttering them up, but the rest of the time taking the mickey out of them so they could never be sure whose side he was really on. He had the time of his life with us. To stir the pot even further, Willy's real feelings about the music were as much a mystery as his views on his audience. One minute he'd be as solemn and reverent and scholarly as you like; next he'd be taking the rise something rotten, perhaps out of the very same song and taking it brilliantly, and what's more teasing us all to death about whether we were wide enough awake to go with him through the change-over. 'You know, some of the ballad survivals are really *weird*,' he'd say in that uncanny attention-grabbing way that instantly had you being *very* careful not to make distracting noises when you breathed, 'even really fragmented survivors. In an awful lot of them, you could swear that the fragmentation has actually increased the weirdness. You know, sort of stripped away all the civilized narrative trappings and left the really quite terrifying raw elemental forces to work on you direct. Like naked Jungian archetypes, *folk*-memories, eh? Maybe from pre-linguistic times? And you find them surviving in bloody lunatic places. Like, you're listening to wee girls skipping or stotting the ball and it suddenly hits you, Jesus Christ, these weans are singing about sibling rape or ritual murder or ritual sibling cannibalism or whatever. Here's a song I bet you could still find old ladies singing in the East End tonight, but even in this form you can't miss the eerie overtones of infanticide, even child sacrifice, perhaps, of the supernatural visitation, of ritual water burial.' By this time we're falling off the edges of our seats. 'It's called,' says Willy, with a *brilliant* little pause to fine-tune his bass string, '"Your Baby Has Gone Down the Plug-hole".'

We all loved it. We must have been bloody masochists, Willy used to say so quite openly, but we all loved it. For a few months that seemed at the time to be going on forever, Willy was the nearest thing to God Incarnate that any of us ever hoped or wanted to see. And there was absolutely no side to him, you know? None of the prima donna. Talk to absolutely anybody when he wasn't actually working, that was all part of the attraction. Everybody's mate, or managing to extend that stage magic to his ordinary conversation so that every-body *felt* like his mate. In all the times I went to that club, I never saw Willy given the chance to put his hand in his pocket to buy a drink, there was always a queue to treat him. And it was seemingly against his nature to risk offence by refusing whenever his glass was empty. If he hadn't had a ferocious head for drink, some of his second sets could have been drunken fiascos. As it was, things did occasionally get a bit, well, *cryptic*. 'A black mamba can samba at the speed of a galloping horse,' Willy once declared out of the blue. Another time he announced he was going to found the Israeli Christian Democrat Party. Or he might suddenly ask, 'Is there a blind photographer in the house?' Or again, 'Anywhere I hang my hat is home, and I never wear a hat.' But all this would be at the stage of the evening where he'd already pulverized the audience for over an hour, and when most of them were so high on booze and admiration he could have had them helpless by reading out the bar tariff. Even three or three-and-a-half sheets to the wind, Willy's judgement and control of his audience stayed spot on.

For all the bonhomie during club hours, Willy always managed to distance himself slightly from most of us outside the boundaries of his performances. For ages, none of us had any real idea what he did for a living – this was quite a few months before the *Melody Maker* folk section small ads showed you he was working four or five club gigs a week, he only had just that one residency, and someone who claimed to know the guy on the door said Willy was only on a flat fiver a night right up to the time he left when the place used to be packed to bursting-point. He must have had some kind of regular job too, but we never found out what it was. If you quizzed him, he'd usually give you some brilliant fantastical answer like, 'I am a professional horse-darkener.' On that first night, I heard him tell Inaudible Adams dead straight-faced at the interval that he was the deputy editor of *Frogs and Frogmen*. Nobody even knew for a long time where he lived. He'd just sort of erupt into our lives for a couple of amazing hours each week and then at closing-time he'd slip quickly downstairs and off into the night in the old shit-coloured Triumph Mayflower he claimed to have bought from a Very Used Car dealer. But a few weeks before he finally jacked it in at the club, he did start to melt a bit. Maybe he'd already had the offer from the record company and knew he'd soon be packing the club in, I don't really know, but he did start to invite a select few of the regulars back to his place afterwards. He only did it four or five times, I suppose, but that's when I first really got to *know* him, to be a friend rather than a fan, you know?

Willy's street was in that bit between the Archway inter-section and Hornsey Rise; Upper Holloway, I suppose you'd call it. It's all been pulled down and built over now. The house Willy lived in was divided off into shabby furnished flats and bedsits. I was never very clear about who lived in which or shared what bathrooms, kitchens and such with who else. Most of the ground floor was shared by some Irish nurses from the Whittington who I never saw as they seemed to be on permanent nights. Willy referred to them darkly as The Biddies and claimed to have nothing to do with them. 'No fear,' he said when asked, 'not with a barge-pole. A fate worse than life, that.' The rest of the house always seemed to be occupied by a vague party crowd when we got there, most of the doors open and lights on and people coming and going all over the place. The population changed quite a bit from week to week, too, and it was a bit of a mystery who actually lived there and who were visitors like us. Willy gently dis-couraged us from asking such questions. 'It's not *polite*,' he told us, 'and you could easy get a very sore face.' A black youth called Pimlico was usually there, grinning and giggling when you spoke to him; Willy claimed he was the illegitimate son of T. L. Essiot, the Chocolate-coloured Coon. There was a big ugly middle-aged Cockney guy with a raspy voice who was always there too. I had him down as a punch-drunk dustman until, years later, it suddenly dawned on me that he was a bit-part character actor I'd seen in 101 ten-second appearances over the years playing himself in Ealing comedies or toothpaste commercials. To this day I have never found out that man's name, do you know that? And there was this really decrepit old drag queen who'd once been something in music hall, looking like Edith Sitwell the morning after and sounding like Walter Gabriel the night before; Albert his right name was. Willy was always beautifully polite to Albert, calling him 'Marchioness' and bowing to kiss his hand. I don't think Albert ever realized Willy was spelling it 'Martianess'. But the rest of the crowd, well, I can't really remember anything after all this time except a whole lot of faces, talking loudly and laughing, mostly.

When I say it was like a permanent party at that house, I wouldn't want you to get the idea of any frenzied celebration or anything. It was a nice easy-going atmosphere, dead friendly and casual, but there was never very much in the way of food or booze and I don't even remember anyone dancing. The only music I ever remember hearing was when Willy played or sang, and you didn't dance to that, you *listened*. But even so, you could really feel the mood of the company lift when the word went round that Willy was home again. Years later, when I thought I'd forgotten all about those days, I came across the film *Tell Them Willie Boy Is Here* in a late night telly repeat, and straight away I was thinking of those few evenings in a scruffy old house in N19. 'Up in Albert's, Willy!' someone would call, or, 'We're in the bridal suite!' And pretty soon most of the house would congregate in somebody's place, and Willy would hold court for as long as he felt like staying awake. There'd be maybe fifteen or twenty people sitting around drinking mostly instant coffee because Willy would've already had enough drink for the night, so he would want coffee and everybody else just wanted to be like Willy. And everybody would just talk and laugh and generally feel good. Willy didn't dominate the proceedings, you know, not in any way you could notice, but he had this talent for getting people to enjoy themselves. 'Oh aye, you're right,' he said once when I asked him about it, 'It's magic. I've got no idea how I do it, but as long as it keeps working I'm not going to worry about that.'

If I had to put my finger on one thing about Willy during those few evenings twenty years and more ago it'd be this: as long as there was even one other person around, Willy seemed obliged to *perform*. He was so bloody good at it that an awful lot of people never noticed it was going on, but it was always there. It was as though unhappy or even slightly bored people presented Willy with an irresistible challenge.

Well, about then Willy got the Transatlantic contract and quit that club residency, and around the same time I had one thing and another to sort out in my personal life which I'll not bore you with, but the end result was that the two of us never got to be really close friends. Willy's name was getting better and better known, and the ticket prices to see him were getting higher and higher, at exactly the same time as the contacts he'd had with our crowd were getting staler and staler, so we weren't even regulars in his audience any more. Over the space of a year or so, I suppose – quite a long time when you're that age – things just drifted to the point where we maybe Knew Him When, but we didn't Know Him Now any more. Mind you, we all still took a fair interest in his progress; even Knowing Him When would have been quite something for us if he'd ever made it really big. He never did, of course, but he kept coming close enough to keep our hopes for him alive for ages. As far as the folk scene went Willy actually was quite big-time, of course, but Willy's own style of folk was only really popular with Joe Public Junior for a matter of a few months. Still, a lot of people who started out from more or less the same time and place as Willy did do rather well for themselves rather quickly, and as time went on

I think we got to feel he was sort of letting us down, cheating us of something that was rightfully ours, almost. At the time, we gradually grew as treacherous as any other public figure's admirers seem to grow if the run is long enough. First we stopped predicting his forthcoming success in favour of gossip about what he was like, then we began to refer to him only in the past tense, then we more or less forgot him.

One day in 1967 (I remember the year all right this time), I was coming out of the V & A at lunchtime when I heard a familiar voice saying, 'No bad for a steel-driving man, eh?' It was Willy, grinning at me. He nodded in the direction of a statue in front of Brompton Oratory. John Henry, Cardinal Newman. Willy had grown his hair a bit and he was wearing jeans, which I'd never seen him do before, but otherwise he looked much as ever. He could probably have said the same about me, except for the jeans. He asked if I wanted a lift, indicating a spotless white V8 Pilot, twenty years old, perhaps, but someone had recently spent an awful lot of time and money on it. 'Investment,' Willy said, patting the bonnet, and drove accordingly, but even at half-throttle she turned heads. I had to get back to the office. Trainee Accountant by day and Raving Loony Head by night was what I'd actually grown up to be by that time. But Willy arranged to meet me after work in Finch's in the Fulham Road and things just sort of started up again from there as if there'd never been a break. There was a middle-aged guy in Finch's in a BOAC pilot's uniform, full fig, paralytic at 6.30. Just after I got there, he was chucked out for playing the bagpipes, much to Willy's amusement. 'Christ, Drew,' he said as the drunken pipes skirled and moaned away down the street, 'you'll not get me up in one of them things.' Same old Willy.

He was living in a house behind the World's End. That's been pulled down and built over too since, come to think of it. (I wonder if there's been some mad bureaucrat in County Hall all these years, whose sole aim in life is to demolish anywhere Willy lives. *What? Who lives there? Willy Soutar? Down with it!* Willy would've enjoyed that notion.) But it was a pretty naff street Willy lived in, not that we'd have said 'naff'. 'Grotty', I expect we'd have said. Willy shared a two up, three down house plus Garden Flat, or coal cellar with the coal taken out and the walls whitewashed. The guys he shared it with were a young guy called Pete, who I never really saw much of but who Willy said was the best story-teller he'd ever heard if you could only catch him sober. This was difficult, because Pete was in the Customs and Excise and worked in a bonded warehouse. He usually tottered in about half past four and went straight to bed to sleep off a hard day's Breakages and Sampling. And there was a guy called Frank who spoke very Ecky Thump, though Willy swore he'd been at Eton. He worked in an estate agent's by day and did up old cars in the back garden in his own time. He was the source of the V8 Pilot. And the other three guys were in Willy's band. Do you know, I'm not sure any more if it was OK to say 'band' in 1967? A few years earlier it definitely wasn't, you had to say 'group'. 'Bands' were grand-dad outfits like Joe Loss and Eric Delaney. Anyway, Willy never seemed to be able to make up his mind what to call the band, and at various stages it was Brake Pedal Down and Bent Frame and Humbly Report and Low Cockalorum. There was a guitarist called Paul and a bass-player called Gordon; they had the same surname which I've forgotten but they weren't related. They went around looking very *wise*, giving the impression that you couldn't possibly shock *them*, they knew everything about everything, only it would be really *uncool*, you know, to ask them about it. The drummer was a big ape-shaped guy called Ogmore and he was a bloody lunatic. You got the impression that the only reason Ogmore wanted all the money in the world was so he could have *really* expensive things to smash up with a clump-hammer or throw in the Thames or sell to someone in the Wetherby public bar for slightly more than the other guy could afford. I liked Ogmore, but Willy didn't. The house was in Ogmore's name, though. Frank had swung that somehow. Frank knew Ogmore from school, I think. It was an unfurnished let, too, the only way you could get security of tenure in those days. Just as well. The neighbours all *hated* those guys. Those guys were really *loud*.

I was at a couple of parties in that World's End house, and you expected that sort of thing to be loudish, but it was the rest of the time that really pissed off the neighbours. Willy was a bloody fanatic for rehearsing, and they weren't working all that much, so those poor neighbours got to hear about a hundred times as much as the rest of the world ever did of that band, and especially Ogmore. Ogmore's head only had the two internal volume settings, Bloody Deafening and A Hell of a Lot Louder than That. The others were forced to crank their own volume level right up to have even an outside chance of hearing themselves. Nobody else had any difficulty at all hearing them for two streets in any direction. Most of the neighbours would have complained to the police, except that most of the neighbours were the sort of people who would cross the street rather than risk having to speak to a policeman. Most of the neighbours must have been really pleased when Willy finally took the band to Spain.

In the six or eight months before that, when they were lucky to work three times a fortnight and lucky to break even on most of those gigs, Willy's spirit never once flagged. Some of the gigs I tagged along to were pretty depressing, too. Student Unions with the audience determined to be hypercool and unimpressed by anything less than a Living Legend, and mostly demonstrating their sophistication by keeping to the bar until the end of the extension. Big dingy pubs in Brentford or Camberwell or Kentish Town, where half the audience would really have preferred Deirdre O'Blarney or topless go-go or 'See The Pyramids Along The

Nile' and talked and laughed and drank right through every number. The band's morale was not helped by the constant bickering between Willy and Ogmore, who used to complain bitterly when Willy refused to let him have his drums miked and amplified. Unamplified acoustic Ogmore was about three times too loud for some of the places the band played, but Ogmore had half-read one of the usual half-garbled interviews in *Melody Maker* or *NME* that had happened to half-mention miking drums, and he was convinced that he was being unjustly cheated of the World-famous Ogmore Sound.

After a few months of this, Paul and Gordon were finding it a bit hard to keep convincing themselves that sitting in the Six Bells trying to decide between three light-and-bitters each or sharing a pound deal from Scotch Jimmy really was so ultracool. 'Dear Mum,' Ogmore used to dictate into his empty half-pint, 'it is really great being a hippy and brilliant musical genius and international superstar of stage, screen and Eamonn Thing, but please send me all the money in the world. *Now*. This is not the first time I have had occasion to write to you about this.' The spirits of Low Cockalorum or Counterfeit Rhinestone or whatever they were called that week were even further depressed by their chronic failure to become international sex-symbols, or even SW10 sex-symbols. The local Mums' Mafia had frightened all their daughters off going near Ogmore's house. The band didn't work often enough to get sated on one-night stands from the audience, and when they did work they were often the support for a name band. It used to drive Ogmore wild when even the name band's roadies got better pickings than he did. 'And another thing, Mum,' he would dictate, 'what the *fuck* happened to the wall-to-wall chicks? A brilliant international musical supergenius is supposed to have wall-to-wall chicks.' Willy would tell him you had to start small and at least they had wall-to-wall ceilings, and Ogmore would say, 'Yeh, well,' in a We-Do-Remember-Whose-Name-The-House-Is-In-Don't-We voice.

The band wasn't half bad, by the way. A lot of name bands were still pretty rough live in 1967, and Humbly Report or Sane Hatter or whatever usually sounded at least as good as the act they were supporting. They knew it, too, which didn't help. But Willy really was amazingly irrepressible. It's hard to describe it, the lift Willy always seemed to be able to give the other guys' spirits whenever yet another day of unfame began to look too much for flesh and blood to stand. But for Willy, that band wouldn't have lasted six weeks.

And then Willy managed to get them a solid deal for six months' work, even if it was in Spain, and I got married and mortgaged and moved to Northwood Hills. A mortgage and commuting from Northwood Hills plays merry hell with being even a part-time Raving Loony Head. Willy and I drifted apart again.

On the day after our divorce became final in 1970, I took a week off work that had been owing me for some time, locked up the empty house and headed up West in search of old friends and lost good times. I had a bad case of chewed nerves and shot digestion from the last six months of wedded bliss and I prescribed myself a complete break. I could afford it. She may have been incompatible but she wasn't greedy, and her new guy was positively loaded. I told myself I wasn't banking on meeting up with Willy – three years is a long break when you're still quite young – but I think that deep inside I didn't really believe what I was telling myself.

I found him four days later in De Hems. I was sitting on a bar stool and the place was pretty dead, when suddenly there was this enormous outburst of coughing and spluttering from one of the booths at the rear, all mixed up with maniacal laughter and voices stage-whispering to each other for quiet. 'I keep telling you,' a familiar voice said with just enough pompous solemnity to provoke helpless giggles from the hidden listener, 'it is against the *law of the land* to smoke these illegal cannabis reefer cigarettes.' Willy. I sneaked up

113

on them and told them they were busted. 'Hullo, Drew,' Willy
says without even turning round. The other guy was Ogmore,
the guy Willy loved to hate. They'd been smoking the world's
longest illegal cannabis reefer cigarette rolled in bright orange
tissue, and from the look of Ogmore he'd been too greedy and
got a lungful of smoke from the end of the two-foot cardboard
tip. 'Birthday,' he wheezes, waving the world's longest roach,
'drink.' I got a round in. Willy was on Southern Comfort with
Mackeson chasers and Ogmore wanted a White Shield 'with
all the bits poured in to watch the look on the geezer's face.'
'Fuckeh nuh-case!' snorts the angry little Chinese barman,
'You tell fahren, he sick he go gence, noh mess floh.'

It turned out that Willy and Ogmore were now number one
buddies. They were sharing a house in Kilburn Park with a
guy who scraped a living out of some obscure agit-prop
organization and a lady Willy swore was called Fat Harry,
who ran a haberdashery and handweave shop called Crewel
Mother in the Chalk Farm Road. This was back before Camden
Market ever got going and Dingwall's was still a dead warehouse, so maybe Fat Harry knew something nobody else did.
I never got to meet her.

(Yes, since you ask. They pulled that one down and built
over it, too.)

Willy had stopped playing by then, except for the occasional
session work to help keep the rent paid. What he was really
trying to break into was independent record production.
'Ach, there's more than one way to skin a cat, Drew.' 'And
none of them's painless,' says Ogmore. Willy spun me tales of
his wheeling and dealing that I couldn't pretend to follow and
that I half-suspected he didn't really want me to follow. 'What
he means,' says Ogmore, 'is he spends his time between
freebies at press shows telling lies in the Admiral Duncan to
geezers claiming to be big wheels at Track Records or the
Dick James Organization and has a running bet with me for
all the money in the world that he can go longer than I can

114

without buying a round. And another thing, Mum,' he dictates into the world's longest roach, 'where you were telling me about if you're not lucky, don't bet. . . '

Willy's Spanish venture had ended in tears of some sort, but Willy made it very clear he didn't want to discuss it. Paul and Gordon were apparently unmentionable. When they chucked us out at ten past three, Ogmore was promptly sick into a small litter-bin on a lamp-post. 'Dear Mum,' he says, poking the lid of the bin open with the world's longest roach, 'should you perchance have been reduced to emptying Soho litter-bins to earn a crust, I have some grave news to impart.' 'Fuckeh nuh-case!' says the triumphant Chinaman locking up De Hems.

Over a triple order of Murgh Massalam (*chicken chest long marineered in orient spice and stuff with delicacy mince meat. A trend dish long popular in India with snob young persons and Royalty*) in Rupert Street, Willy again expounded his current plans. Ogmore ate most of the food. 'I *hate* food,' Ogmore says between shovelfuls, 'I only eat it to be polite. See, I just can't *stand* the sight of it there on the plate. And what else polite can you do with it?' Willy claimed to have sussed out that American record companies had started quietly falling over themselves to pay out massive advances to British bands for two- or three- or five-album deals on the off-chance of hitting the jackpot. All you had to do was get to the right guy at the right time with the right sales pitch. 'But you know what homes in on that sort of money, Drew. Scum of the fucking earth. There's *Mafia* guys getting into the music business. You know, real tone-deaf Nice-a Legs You Gotta There, Pity If Anything Happen To Them guys.' 'Madre mia,' says Ogmore into the water jug, 'paranoia she ees so *fashionable* thees year. . .' Willy *was* just a touch obsessional about the possibility of getting screwed. 'What makes me wild, Drew, is here I am knowing all there is to know about putting good music together. I'm not boasting. There's more in this

115

head than some of those Harvard Business School bastards could learn if they spend the rest of their lives taking lessons. They come on with all this 'Cool, man' and 'Outasight' shit, but I know their game. If I don't watch them like a bloody hawk, *my* deal that *I've* put together gets hijacked by some fly bastard tone-deaf lawyer or accountant. Oh, sorry Drew, I forgot,' and I ended up having to tell him the old chestnut about an accountant being a man professionally qualified to prove that the pieces of string are the length the boss needs them to be before I could convince him I wasn't offended.

The evening (it turned into an evening) was a relaxed upbeat affair, with Willy on top of his form and making very optimistic noises about his beloved deal. The only unpleasant moment was when I casually asked if they still saw Frank and Ogmore nearly bit my head off. 'Frank's dead, Drew,' says Willy, 'last year, car crash. Ogmore doesn't like to talk about it. Never mind, Ogmore, time is a great healer. We're working on the side-effects.'

I couldn't tell you why, but neither Willy nor I made any very serious effort to stay in touch after that meeting. I once got a Get Well Soon card from LA signed 'Millicent Fuckpig' in Willy's handwriting, but I've no idea to this day what he was doing over there. And it could only have been Willy who sent me the 'Whatever Happened to Urea Hype?' album that must now be a very rare item indeed, because I think there was some monumental fuck-up with the distribution deal and I never ever saw or heard another copy of it. But one way or another, it was a good five years before we met again face to face.

We'd been to dinner at some friends in Islington, and they took us out to a pub in Upper Street to round the evening off. Good band, they said. And I think the band with a thousand names that Willy had back in the sixties would have given their eye-teeth for a venue like that instead of those God-awful indifferent music lounges in Catford and Stratford and

Edmonton. These punters actually came to the place *for* the music, and they sat and listened to it. And applauded. It was a tiny stage, or a big shelf really, and the place was pretty packed. The only seats we could get were off to one side, and one of the guitarists was hidden from us by the upright piano that looked like it came with the pub rather than the band. He was the one doing the announcements and, of course, it was Willy Soutar. 'This next number,' he says, 'is something like a rag and something like a jig. We were thinking of calling it a rig. Or a jag. But then the sky fell on us, so it's called "Turkey Lurkey in the Straw".' The crowd were lapping him up, and the band *was* good. 'This next one is the school song of the Dublin Tightrope Academy, where they do the mick stability teaching.' The atmosphere was very relaxed, almost like the old folk club days. It looked like Willy Soutar might have found his real audience at last. He came and had a drink at our table during the interval. He was living 'in bandit country south of the river and north of the Wandsworth Road, where they vandalize the graffiti and the regular weekly housebreaker nails down anything he can't steal, including the householder. *Especially* the householder. All human life is there and Millwall FC supporters.'

(If it hasn't been pulled down, someone should be ashamed of themselves.)

He was half a stone heavier and starting to get thin on top, but he still managed to look younger than I'd seen him do for maybe ten years. 'You see before you a happy man, Drew,' he says, 'I've stopped *running*, Drew. And you know what? I found out there was no bugger chasing me in the first place.' I asked after Ogmore and Willy's face clouded for a second. 'Dead, Drew,' he says, 'three years dead. We bummed around the Outer Hebrides a few months together, did you know? One of Ogmore's contacts got us a Trinity House contract painting unmanned lightships and towers. Ogmore's idea was we'd make all the money in the world by only painting

117

the sides you could see from the shore and flogging off the rest of the paint. But the silly bastard never told me he couldn't swim, can you credit it? Some of the jobs we were doing, I wished we had lifejackets. Christ, some of them, I wished we had parachutes and a lifeboat. But he survived all that and then fell off the jetty pissed one night on his way back to the tent. The body came back with the tide three days later. I miss old Ogmore, Drew, but only when I think about it.' The moment passed. Willy brightened up again and left us to start the second set. We managed to squeeze a place round where we could see him. He'd put on an *enormous* pair of shades and sat down at the piano. He played a long loud bluesy flourish to shut the crowd up, then the band joined in as he went into the introduction to the Ray Charles version of 'Georgia On My Mind'. He bent to the mike. You could almost literally have heard the proverbial pin. *'Georgia,'* he sang, *'Porgia. . .'*

That was a good second set. No, it was a *great* second set. I've never thought of it till now, but I think that evening was the longest spell I ever had of pure unmitigated *happiness*, you know, the kind you're consciously aware of at the time. There was no doubt about it, Willy Soutar was going to be OK.

It wasn't all that long after that that rock music really went to hell in a handcart as far as I was concerned. I even gave up listening to John Peel, he was playing so much shit. You know, the *gotnojob/gotnofewcha/gotnoearfor/FUCKINMUSIC* school. I decided if that was what the kids were into, I was a permanent grown-up. And what with that, and moving house around that time, and our own two growing up and the like, I wasn't taking too active an interest in the career of W. Soutar. but whenever I did think of him, I *knew* that W. Soutar was doing just fine.

Then about a year ago, I was sitting here on this stool about 6 o'clock when a whole bunch of really heavy-looking guys all came in together, total strangers. Most of them looked like they'd failed the audition for the All-England Chapter of Hell's Angels because they'd made the Angels nervous. I thought we'd been invaded by some new species of Nightmare Biker, but it turned out they were some of the road crew from the Helen Damnation 'Why Put The Bomp?' tour at the Odeon. And Willy Soutar was with them. Most of them went through to the games room to encourage the pool players and frighten the living shit out of the Donkey Kong machine, but Willy spotted me and brought one of them over to chat. Have you ever noticed how every ageing skinhead looks just about to evolve into a really evil club bouncer, but no really evil club bouncer actually looks like he's ever been a skin? The guy with Willy was the really evil bouncer who was the exception to that rule. 'Meet Captain Beefbrain,' says Willy, 'my right-hand Thing.' 'How do, John,' says the Captain. The Captain appeared to be a brain-free zone, though the faint gleam in his eye suggested he might, just *might* be putting you on. 'When some punter wants to get really heavy,' says Willy, 'I just point the Captain at them and *whop*. Instant Steak Tartare.' Willy was on Perrier, the Captain was drinking pints of snakebite. Very quickly. It turned out that Willy was security boss. 'Ach, it was that or the dole or going into publishing with this guy starting up the Dyslexic Necrophile Press. It's a living. I've got philosophical about that sort of thing, Drew. You have to be philosophical.' 'It's a laugh,' says the Captain, halfway down his third pint, 'really mega. Free music and you get to hit people *and* they pay you.' As well as philosophical, Willy had got fat. Well, what the hell, so have I. But it looked *good* on Willy, it really did. Impressive. 'When the Captain grows up, he wants to be a special effect,' says Willy. The Captain nodded agreement. 'I used to think he might be the runaway son of a noble house, but then I caught him eating oxtail soup with a *fishfork*.' Willy was talking a blue streak despite the temperance bevy, but it looked like just pure nervous energy rather than anything from Boots or elsewhere. 'Hey, nobody died, Drew,' he says, 'I usually only get to meet this guy again after somebody dies, you know?' He was telling one joke after another so quickly that there was hardly time to take them in, and it was pretty clear that Captain Beefbrain was the world's number one W. Soutar fan. I asked Willy where he was living. 'Any place I hang my head is home,' he says. I asked what Ms Damnation was like to work with. 'Bloody prima donna,' he says, 'thinks she's got a field marshal's baton in her shoulder-bag. Walks like she's got one up her arse.' The Captain thought that one was a killer. I asked Willy if he never felt jealous of some of the fairly talent-free names at the top just recently. He said not. He said he was too old and too wise for being a rock'n'roll star. 'And Grandpaw Soutar's advice to the young is to get your youth over and done with while you still can.' Willy couldn't seem to shut himself up and he was still yammering away when the word came through to the Captain from the games room that snakebite break was over. (Seven, in about fifty minutes. He slowed down badly in the last quarter of an hour.) Willy was still joking away as he shepherded his crew out the door, and I can't remember the last thing I heard him say, but it seemed very quiet in here when they'd gone. I do remember thinking, *I may not want to be you when I grow up any more, Willy Soutar, and you may be getting a bit frayed at the edges, but you still make me feel good.*

Then came that piece in last night's *Standard*. It was the inquest report; I'd somehow managed to miss any earlier coverage of the death itself, even though it must have been fairly lurid stuff on the lines of *Horrified passengers watched as the 5.17 Euston express drew into Watford Junction with the body of a man impaled on the front of the engine*. Willy Soutar, no doubt at all, even a picture of him. The engine driver hadn't seen a thing. Suicide. The man I once wanted to be. Mr Soutar had been unemployed for nine months, it said, and had a medical history of repeated treatment for depression and alcoholism. And worse than that. SIXTH TIME UNLUCKY, the headline read. He had first attempted suicide at boarding school, it said. In 1965 he had been rescued from the Thames at Chelsea Reach after apparently jumping from a houseboat. In 1968 he had spent three months in hospital following a fall in mysterious circumstances from a third-floor hotel room in Barcelona. In 1973 he had taken a drug overdose following the death of a close friend in a drowning accident. In 1979 he had been voluntarily treated for depression following another overdose. At the time of his death, the social report said, Mr Soutar had been living alone and seemingly had no close friends.

Willy Soutar?

No close friends?

When I was very young, I had a really bad time with dogs. I don't remember how it started; probably some well-meaning grown-up trying to warn me that some dogs bite, but by the time I was five and six and seven, I *knew* that all the dogs in the world were *after* me. And of course, the stupid thing is that any dog that senses you *know* that really will go for you. I had a bad time with dogs when I was five and six and seven. Sure enough, I grew out of it, but even now, whenever I'm feeling a bit down or the old self-confidence has taken a bit of a bashing, one of the first things I notice is that I start to get nervous about dogs again. Ever since I read that *Standard* item last night and the whole thing started to go round and round in my head, I have not looked forward one bit to meeting any unaccompanied dogs. But now I've told it to you, I feel better. I still don't understand any of it, but I do believe it, and any more thinking I do on the subject will be voluntary. On the way home tonight, I won't be crossing the road for any dog.

Here's another true thing for you out of the *Standard* report, from the train driver's evidence. He didn't see anything or feel any impact, which isn't surprising when you consider the relative weights of W. Soutar and the 5.17 Euston express. It'd be like you or me on a push-bike hitting a money-spider. He did hear something, though. A small, hollow sound, only just real, he said. He didn't do anything about it at the time because he thought he knew what it was. He thought it was the sound the drivers hear when the train collides at speed with a bird in flight.

ALMOST GRACEFUL LIKE A DANCER

For Dave and Siobhan Stenhouse

Ah, but it was a different world then entirely. The times are that changed nowadays; sometimes I feel like I am a native born of those old times but only an immigrant and a stranger in the present day. I'll tell you a thing puts what I mean right in a nutshell. Just about then, just after the old great-aunt died, that was the time when all the fashion and the rage was for the folk music, or what people were pleased to call folk music. There was hardly a pub in London with an upstairs room for hire that didn't have some class of folk club or other meeting there, and any fool with half a voice and enough gall could learn ten songs and get away with calling himself a folk singer. The McCarthy that was site agent of the first job I worked on, he ran a club of his own above a pub behind Clapham Junction; I was down there myself a few times. The crack was fair enough, except the draught was thrown at you when they got busy, and that at a public bar price to equal most saloons round this way. But it was an awkward old journey, not far in distance, but awkward with the changing and that, and there were places every bit as good within walking distance of the digs here. Anyway, the point I was wanting to make to you was that there was nobody more popular round the folk-singing clubs at that time than Irish Paddy, provided he laid off the Percy French and swore he got all his songs from his mother. And the most popular Irish Paddy of the lot of them was the boy with the rebel songs. Many's the time I've sat in one of these clubs and watched the young warriors strutting on the platform with the sleeves of their jumpers rolled back to the elbow because that's what the Clancy Brothers did, whaling the bejasus out of their guitars and proclaiming themselves to be the Boys of Wexford or asking in martial tones for the news from the bold Shelmalier with his long-barrel gun from the sea. Nine times out of ten when they made the announcements between songs they were pure Cockney, and this at a time when half the youth of Ireland were mad to get singing in a showband sounding like Jim Reeves or Frankie Laine. It was all you could do to keep a straight face. The entire town was infested with Behans and Dubliners and God knows what all. There was never a better time to be Irish in London, nor ever will be again. And on the fiftieth anniversary of the Easter Rising, do you know what they did? They had an entire programme on the English television on nothing but the old rebel songs, 'Erin go Bragh', 'I am a Jolly Ploughboy', 'Foggy Dew', 'Sergeant William Bailey Tooraloo', the blooming lot of them, all done by Irish singers. I ask you, could that happen today? It could not.

Even the work is not the same today, and I don't just mean there's less of it about. What do these young fellows today know? The better part of them would be killed stone dead if they had to do a proper day's hard graft. What do they know or care about serving your time at a trade? If I was a piece of four by two, I would be insulted to have some of these cowboy chippies today so much as look at me. And what's worse, there is no character or spirit in them. When I was their age, you could find more characters on a single job than they could get together today from every site in London. Even Danny Lenihan that you can see any day of the week with the other dossers drinking their sherry and meths below the railway arches, even Danny has been man enough to go to hell in his own good time and no complaints, and in his younger days he could have given any of this crowd a half-mile start and a beating for character and spirit.

Block o' Wood, now, there was a character for you. Big Francie Power, to give him his right name, the best subbie me and Danny ever worked for. Never once failed to see us right. A very slow-spoken man and always the queer dead expression on his face the way you might think he was slow-witted if you didn't know him. Two Scotch boys that we done some roofs with, it was them first started calling him Block o' Wood behind his back, and the rest of us waiting for the balloon to go up when Francie caught them at it. He was bound to catch them sooner or later for no matter how slow he might look, Francie Power had an eyes and an ears on him and missed nothing whatsoever. And for all that he was no longer young, he was not a man you would choose to anger, a great strong rawboned fellow that played for Tip in an all-Ireland final before the war. So when the evil thing finally happened you could have heard a pin drop, and the rest of us wondering whether the two Jimmies were going to be let keep their heads on their shoulders, but your man does nothing only let go a great laugh. 'Hurrah ha *ha*!' he cries, 'Block o' Wood! A name among names!' 'Oh, aye, ah, you're no offended then, Jimmy?' says one of the Scotch boys. 'Not a bit of it,' says your man as slow and pleasant as you like, 'a grand name, and long may I live to bear it. You're both sacked.' Anyway, nobody on a building site ever called him anything but Block o' Wood after that, and himself as happy as Larry about it. It suited him fine, do you see, for certain of the people he'd be doing business with to be thinking they were only dealing with a Tick Irish Paddy. Block o' Wood was nobody's fool, and that's a fact.

Jesus, they were some great times we used to see working for Block o' Wood. You never minded the graft when there was such great crack to go with it, and such desperate characters. Gauger Peasely, now, did you never meet the Gauger? Your life is the poorer for it, for there was never another man like him. 'After they made me, they broke the mould,' says the Gauger one time. 'Away,' says Danny Lenihan, 'it was making you that broke the poor bastard.' 'Not a bit of it,' says Block o' Wood, 'they broke the mould *before* they made him.' 'Ah, go and bah-boil yourselves,' says the Gauger. You could never call the Gauger a well-made man, at any road. A head on him like a small horse, and clapped on to the body of a lightweight jockey the way you'd swear they had a mix-up at the factory. He had a great harsh voice on him as rough as emery-board, and a real terrible stutter. 'Gauger,' says Block o' Wood one day, 'there in your throat you have the world's one and only stuttering frog. Could you not train it to do a few circus tricks and live a life of ease yourself?' 'Ah, tah-tie a knot in yourself,' the Gauger says. Still, he was a good little grafter, only he was that wandery in his mind sometimes that you'd need the likes of Block o' Wood to be sure of getting a hand's turn out of him.

I remember one time when we were gutting the top two floors of a house in Canonbury on a flats conversion. We had a skip to fill in a bit of a hurry due to Block o' Wood being on a price to finish it that same day. We had a platform hoist up to a knocked-out window on the second floor and I was working that from above. You should always work a hoist from above the way you can see is there anyone on the platform, but half these young know-alls today cannot be told and that's how most accidents happen, in my opinion. The Gauger was down on the ground and his job was to take the full barrow of rubbish for the skip off the hoist and put the barrow he'd already emptied to come back up on the platform. We'd worked up a good old rhythm and the job was going nice and smooth. A hard dirty job like that goes twice as easy if you get a rhythm going and never have to stop and think what to do next; you'd be surprised what a difference it makes. But of course if you once go and break that rhythm, there's hell to pay, and isn't that just what happened? It was maybe the fourth or fifth full barrow I sent down, and the Gauger himself already standing waiting with the empty one at the foot of the hoist. Well, the platform strikes the bottom with a great loud clatter as per usual, and myself with a hand on the lever ready to bring her straight back up the minute the Gauger has switched the barrows, but he makes no move whatsoever. At first I'm thinking he's maybe spotted something amiss with the hoist and I'm giving him a shout to ask what's the matter, but still he doesn't budge. Right you be, I'm thinking, if you want to play the giddy goat, here's one boy will let you get on with it, and I'm for lighting myself a fag while you sort yourself out. But pretty soon the rest of them above start giving it the loud bejasus and worse. The rhythm is broken to hell, do you see, with no barrow to cart away their rubbish from under their feet. And next thing there's Block o' Wood's great turnip head sticking out the top floor window, and him seeing straight off what the trouble is. 'Ahoy the Gauger!' he shouts, 'Is it counting the wheels on your bloody barrow you are, or what?' And *still* not a move from your man on the ground. Block o' Wood gives out a noise like a stallion spoiling for a fight and goes haring away down the stairs. Ah, Gauger dear, I'm thinking to myself, you are a dead man now. But just as Block o' Wood gets to the front door, the Gauger suddenly lets rip with a terrible yell that stops your man in his tracks. At first I was sure the Gauger was in mortal pain, but then I seen the great big grin on him as per usual and him giving me a small wink with the eye farthest from Block o' Wood. 'I have it, Tommy boy!' he roars up at me, 'I *hah-have* it! The winner of the One Thousand Guineas Stakes and not a shah-shadow of a doubt, and me with a memory like a garden riddle and nah-nothing to write with. Could you give me a lend of a pen, or a pah-pencil, or tah-two thousand pah-pounds?' And straight away all the rage in Block o' Wood comes out instead in a great hoot of a laugh, and he goes on laughing and laughing until the tears are streaming down his face and he's gasping for breath, and the Gauger all the while making out he thinks your man's gone demented.

But the spirit of the times is different altogether nowadays,

and we all know what's at the back of that, don't we? For all
that we mightn't talk about it, we all know what's at the back
of that. Things are never going to be quite the same in our
lifetime for the Irishman in London, not even in a place like
this where there's never been any real bother. This was never
really what you might call an Irish house. There's always
been a steady Irish custom here, but it's been the class of Irish
like myself who'd rather get away from the ceilidh bands and
Provo raffles and auctions of autographed photos of the Price
sisters you might have found not so long ago in certain
upstairs rooms in pubs no great distance from here. But do
you remember that time they put the bombs in those pubs in
Birmingham and all those people were killed, young girls and
everything blown to bits? Even in here there was a terrible
atmosphere then. Fairly busy for the early evening when I
came in, but the atmosphere was nobody's business. It was
like everyone was forcing themselves to relax and enjoy the
drink, but the falsehood of the enjoyment showed up in the
quick nervous way they all turned their heads to see who it
was every time the door went. Remember, this was at a time
when there had already been bomb scares enough and real
bombs too so that not only your Englishman was looking a
bit chary at the stranger with the Irish accent, there was many
a London Irishman with the self-same notion in his head.
Myself, I was heartily sickened by that Birmingham business,
and at a complete loss to know what I could possibly say in an
Irish accent that would help things at all. I mean, what on
earth could you say? There was a Dublin gobshite of a bar-
cellarman working here at the time; he done a bunk not three
weeks later at 8 o'clock one night with ninety quid out the till,
but that's another story. He had the running of this bar that
evening until the part-timers came on at half past seven, and I
swear to God you could count that man's brains on the
fingers of one mitten. He was playing it for all he was worth
to try and make out he was on the side of Right, that he was

filled with the same righteous anger as what he seemed to think any Englishman would be. Hanging was too good for the murdering swine, tie them up to ten pounds of gelignite then light the fuse in front of their eyes, you know the class of talk, but all this in a Jackeen accent thick enough to bake bricks out of. You poor bloody donkey, I was thinking, you might as well up and give them a chorus of 'The Boys from the County Cork' for all the good you're doing yourself or the atmosphere in here. I just kept myself to myself and stood having a read of the paper at the end of the bar as per usual. The company was mostly in small groups of two or three, each group having its own conversation, no music or anything that early in the evening.

And then Block o' Wood came in. Now at this time, you understand, I hadn't worked for Block o'Wood for maybe four or five years – no big split-up or ill feeling, mind, it was just that our two lives had gone along different ways. Any road, I wasn't all that surprised when your man walked straight past me without a word, for in the normal way we might not speak to each other once in a twelvemonth. I just went on with my reading and didn't see anything unusual in the way he walked down the bar and stood at the far end of the counter over there. But when I heard him order a brandy and port along with his pint, I had a good look at him, for that was something he only drank when he was on a skite. He looked to be far from sober, but he was behaving himself as nice as you like and I went back to my paper, not wanting to get involved. You can never tell when a man in drink might suddenly drag you into an argument, and I was never an argumental class of man. Well, he just had the one pint, but he must have had four or five short ones in the half-hour he took to drink it and he had quite a sway on him by that time, leaning on the counter with his hands to steady himself. I'd thought he was getting ready to leave the way he put down his glass, but just then there was one of those little lulls in the general conversation of the bar and he spoke straight out into mid-air. 'Ireland,' says Block o' Wood, and the temperature in here went down ten degrees. He hadn't spoken that loud for him, but he had a deep boomy carrying class of voice and the whole room heard him. Your man was standing there staring into space and the rest of the company ignoring him as hard as they could; their own conversations had suddenly become utterly fascinating to them. But I was watching him all right, and I could see there was a tear running down his cheek, just the one tear. And I'm telling you, that one small drop of water transformed the big dead face of Block o' Wood into a mask, a mask of hurt. The life lighting up his eyes kept drifting away and then coming back again; it was like someone was working one of them dimmer switches inside his head. Oh Francie, I thought, I know where you are, poor man, for amn't I there myself? I could almost hear his poor befuddled brains trying to puzzle things out and set themselves to rest. The big rough farm boy from Tipperary, the brave Gaelic footballer, the hard man on the building site, the two-fisted fire-breathing drinking man, he had himself destroyed and defeated altogether trying to make some class of sense out of the world. All his spirit and his pride was awash in a flood of confusion and shame and helplessness, and him only adding to it by pouring a small ocean of drink on top of it. The sway on him was getting pretty bad by now and I thought for a second he was going to fall down, but the light in his eyes came back on yet again and he spoke once more. 'Ireland', he said loud and clear this time, 'will be *free*.' The whole bar was struck silent for a second and people sneaked looks at Block o' Wood out the corners of their eyes, then all the conversations started themselves up again with lots of extra tuttings and hissings to begin with. 'For God's sake, Francie, none of that in here,' says the gobshite, 'will I ring you a cab?' 'I can walk fine,' says Block o' Wood, squaring himself up to leave. Well, he got about halfway down the bar when his legs went, the way he could only save himself from falling by grabbing hold of the shoulder of the man next him, who happened to be Georgie Varley. Do you know Georgie? Big fat fellow keeps a lock-up wet fish shop near the post office. Now anyone with an ounce of sense knows the best way to handle a troublesome man far gone in drink is to jolly him out of it with smiles and pats on the back and such like. Normally, that's how they would have dealt with Block o' Wood, for he was well enough liked in here and a good spender, but as I say, there was a terrible atmosphere in here that night. Instead of making some sort of joke out of it, Georgie just says very sharp, 'Leave it out!' Block o' Wood was leaning on him, swaying, trying to puzzle out what was going on. I maybe could have smoothed things over even then if I'd stepped in, but I'm ashamed to say I couldn't bring myself to do it. 'You,' says Block o' Wood to Georgie, 'I'll punch you right in the fucking nose!' '*Gerroff*,' says Georgie, giving a shrug, no more than a shrug. But Block o' Wood had already drawn his fist back and overdone it and the shrug was enough to destroy his balance entirely. He went teetering away across the room taking those stupid little drunk man's steps like his laces were tied together, weaving this way and that so he looked real comical but at the same time almost graceful like a dancer, and then he fell. He'd passed out cold on his feet, for he never lifted a finger to save himself, and his head came down a terrible bang on the glass front of the electric bandit.

I went to help him then all right. He was spark out and twitching, and there was blood everywhere the way the Jackeen phoned for the ambulance straight off before he ever came round the bar to look. And it's a funny thing, but all the bad atmosphere went the second they could see how bad Block o' Wood was hurt. I heard afterwards he needed twenty-three stitches. Now it was easy to see that your man would have no memory of any of this when he woke up next day, and God knows what class of cock and bull story Danny

Lenihan and the Gauger got, but the pair of them were in here two nights later looking for Georgie Varley to give him a good kicking. It was all the landlady could do to talk sense into them, by all accounts. But Block o' Wood never again crossed that threshold, not even years later. He died not two months ago, you know, the old Block o' Wood. Heart gave up on him, and him not yet sixty.

Was I telling you about the McCarthys' club in Clapham? The Crubeen, he used to call it, after the pig's trotter. There was a picture of a pig on the wall done in that powdery poster paint the kids use in school, a fine fat pink pig with a balloon coming out its mouth saying, 'Crubeen my foot.' I was on a demolition job in Lavender Hill last week, first time in years and years I was down that way, and I thought I'd maybe have a pint in that pub for old times sake. And do you know what? I couldn't even find the blooming street. Acres and acres ripped down and buried under tower blocks and primary schools and new old people's places and them queer shops and libraries and such that look like glorified greenhouses. And not done recently, either. There was a young fellow there selling fruit of a barrow and I tried to explain to him what I was looking for. 'Never happened, John,' he says, 'no way. Lived round here all my life, ain't I? Never nothing like that round here.' True what they say: all the same in a hundred years. It's a hard life, sure enough, but it's the only one there is.

STUNNING THE PUNTERS

For Derek Reid

It's a rough old estate. Be about that time when me and Spike – this whole thing I'm telling you about was his idea really, but we'll get to that in a minute – we'd just come out the entrance of our block; we was hanging about on the front steps arguing the toss about where to go and *wham*, there's this really terrific fucking crash right behind us. Know what it was? Only a pram. Right, a real old-fashioned metal pram, with the big wheels and the spring suspension and everything, smashed to fucking bits. 'Fuckers must have pushed it off the roof,' says Spike, 'far too fucking big to go through them windows.' Fourteen floors, straight down. 'Ten points,' I says to Spike, 'got to be a maximum.' 'Nah,' says Spike 'only get a maximum for a pram if the baby's still in it.' As it happens, that was about the last real pram I ever seen. All them collapsibles and these back-to-front papoose things nowadays, isn't it, with the baby bouncing about getting suffocated in its mother's tits. Expect you'd only get a maximum for one of them if the mother was still wearing it.

Spike's the one who should be telling you all this, Jack the lad, old Spike, but that's impossible the way things turned out, isn't it? Still, you'll be all right with me, got a good memory, I have. Only one out of the lot of us got any O-levels, and that was just from remembering a lot of stupid stuff without really trying. I used to listen to people talking and practise remembering what they said, you know. You ever do that? Really listen to what people say, when they're talking to each other, not to you, I mean? I used to do it because I like to imitate people, take the piss out of them, used to make old Spike cry laughing, I did. And I'll tell you one thing I noticed, you can't take the mickey properly unless first of all you got them down exact, all the details. People really do say amazing fucking things to each other, though. Like, there was these two drunks in here a couple of weeks ago, middle-aged geezers in good suits, and one of them was at the stage where he can't be told nothing, and he keeps saying, 'I don't give a trot. Not a *trot*.' And a bit later on, they're ripping some other geezer to shreds, and the same one says, 'He doesn't know his arse from tuppence.' Then again, coming home tonight on top of the 41 through Crouch End, this old couple was sitting in front, pair of fatties, him in an Andy Capp and she looks like someone's gran. The thing I noticed was, whatever he says, she just nods and goes, 'Hm hm hm hm hm.' Five times, always exactly five times. Most of what he's saying is dead boring, hang the lot of them, price of fags, bleeding unions, and I'm just thinking about joining in the next Hm hm hm hm hm bit, but all of a sudden, in the exact same tone of voice and everything, he goes, 'I wish I was more like Jesus Christ so's I'd be less like Judas Iscariot.' 'Hm hm hm hm hm.' Not a flicker, she's heard it a million times. ''Course, there's electricity all around us,' he says, 'in the air, and through your bones and brains and blood and everything.' 'Hm hm hm hm hm.' Nine points, I thinks, and a maximum if they keep it up till the Hale, but they got off just past the Black Boy in West Green Road.

To get back to what you was asking about, I still reckon it was really them that started it. The blacks, I mean. We got on all right with them for years, didn't we? I mean, we used to call them samboes and they used to call us honkies, but it was all a laugh, nothing meant. Oh, our old man was always going on about blackies this, Pakis that, but we never paid him no mind any more than we did over anything else. The Beer-gut That Walks Like A Man, Kenny used to call him. But there was never anything really nasty between us and the blacks as far as the kids was concerned. I mean, half the faces on the

North Bank was black. At least. And when me and Spike and Alf Rabaiotti got nicked the day we took Millwall, Piggy Mackintosh got nicked right alongside us, and Piggy's as black as Newgate's knocker. When the punks first started and they was rolling into school with the green and pink hair and that, the blacks was on the same side as us skins, you know. Actually used to join in and help us kick shit out of the stupid fucking wimps. They was normal, then, just like us, loved a good ruck. That's another thing that gets me, when people on the telly and that are going on about riots and rucks and things, and they're trying to tell you kids do that stuff because of unemployment, got no valid means of self-fulfilment, alienated from adult society and all that *New Society* shit they used to push at us in Social Studies. That's a load of fucking bollocks. You don't do it because of that. You do it because it's *fun*. How can you be so stupid that you can't twig that? Anyway, I reckon it was the blacks who cut themselves off from the rest of us in the first place, at least as far as the kids was concerned. It was that Rasta shit done it. You know, the dreadlocks and the stripy woollen hats and Hai-Jai-Rastafari and the stupid fucking chug-a-lug-a-Babylon music. All of a sudden, the blacks are all off in their own special bit of the playground, and most of them won't even speak to whitey, them as ain't too spliffed to speak at all. It's like making out we hate them somehow makes them feel more important or something. Like when little kids create because they'd rather get belted by Mum than ignored, maybe. I think what really brought it home was Piggy Mackintosh. Piggy Mackintosh was born next door to me, shut your eyes when he's speaking and you wouldn't know what colour his face was. But one day I'm walking down by Bruce Grove station and Piggy comes up and goes, 'Wot de raarss time, mon, mi fokkin bitch watch losting free minutes a hour.'

Anyway, after a bit, Spike says, 'Fuck this, I'm going to join the National Front.' I tells him he's only doing it to take the piss out of his old man, and I still think that's the truth. Spike's a yid, isn't he? I mean a real yid, a Jewish one, or at least a lapsed Jewish one, not some stupid fucking wally from Tottenham Supporters' Club. His old man sells kosher butchery and stuff down Stamford Hill, and he's got the full rig, black hat, whiskers, the lot. And Spike's always taking the piss out of him, like telling him he's turning vegetarian but not to worry, Dad, going to insist on ritually slaughtered vegetables. And when he first got the skinhead cut, he tells him it's because all his life he's wanted to hear someone say to him, that's funny, you don't look Jewish. Truth is, even before the skinhead hairdo, Spike looks about as Jewish as Bjorn Borg.

But Spike insists he's serious, and he starts bringing NF mags and stuff to school and flyposting and that. And pretty soon he's got Alf Rabaiotti and Denny Plumb and Barry Crump and one or two of the other skins to join the Front, but not me. I don't believe in joining things, do I? But I still knock around with the lads, same as usual. And I don't know what sort of stuff they're pumping into Spike and the rest down the NF, but it seems to me like Spike's getting some sort of Great British Hero complex or something. He's saying stuff like we got to stop all this talk about how we ain't real hard skins like the old days, people saying there ain't been a proper skinhead since Slade let their hair grow, saying we're just a bunch of wimps with short haircuts talking hard to each other to forget how scared we really are. And he's saying there's no class in having rucks with wallies like punks and mods, what we got to concentrate on is getting stuck into the jigaboos. All this is happening just as we're finishing our last year at school, by the way. Most of us just bunked off after the exams were finished, and Alf Rabaiotti bunked off while they were still on. Alf's a tasty geezer in a bundle on account of being so fast and together and built like a rhino, but bright he ain't. But it gets to the point where Spike ain't satisfied with making life hard for the odd solo coon on the street, he's actually got us all going back to school for the sole purpose of having a go at them in strength. So there we all are, mob-handed, stomping along the playground in the old Doc Martens singing these anti-sambo songs Spike either made up or learnt down the NF, like 'Hit the Frog', 'Wog', and 'Haile Selassie's a Bonny Hielan' Lassie' and they don't like it one bit. And we're giving them the old Blubberlips and Wanker signs, and in the end they rush us and there's one really terrific fucking ruck, grief and claret all over the shop. And they're real hard, some of them, but we're still really taking them apart when some-one says the Old Bill's been called and we has to run for it. 'Really good, what?' I says to Spike. 'Nine points?' 'Nah,' he says, grinning all over his face, 'no dead.' And he's laughing and running at the same time, proper nutty-looking, all the wimps on the street getting out of his way like he's a runaway bus. And a funny thing strikes me while we're still running, but I don't tell Spike because I think it might go down wrong. What I'm thinking is, here's Spike and them going on about jungle bunnies and lower forms of life, animals and that, but the only way we was able to take them blacks was to go more animal then they could, how about that? And I'm starting to wonder how much of this race stuff the lads really believe in or is it just an excuse to go mad and have fun spreading grief, but it's best to keep shtum about that sort of thinking or someone's going to get the idea you're a *smart* sod, and *wallop*.

Off and on, we done that sort of caper most of that summer. Got ourselves barred from quite a few pubs and places, destroyed a few happy evenings at concerts and clubs and that. Spike and some of the rest were all tooled up to go on one of them big NF marches, but the law called it off at the last minute. I don't know about the other lads, but after a couple of months of it I'm secretly starting to find it all a bit tedious. Spike seems fidgety, too, and it's about this time he comes up with the stunt you was really asking about.

We was sitting in the boozer one night quite late, bored stiff, trying to come up with something to do that don't cost nothing, due to we're all boracic. Barry Crump says that last week the bouncer in that pub near the Angel Road Community Centre put Jimmy Tollington in hospital, so why don't we trundle over to Edmonton and send the sod on a long sickie, but you can see his heart ain't really in it. There's just the five of us, Barry, Spike, Alf Rabaiotti, Denny Plumb and me. Spike's acting like he's half asleep, but all of a sudden he perks up and starts getting ready to leave. 'Come on, children,' he says, 'we're off to stun the punters.' And he won't tell us where we're going or why, but we tag along because we know Spike and Spike seems to be fair bursting to get at whatever the great secret is. First off we need some transport, he tells us, and at that time we can probably scrape together two-thirds of a dead Honda 90 between the lot of us, so we have to nick a car. Sorry. Take it away and drive it without the owner's consent. 'Denny,' says Spike, 'can you take away and drive without the owner's consent some wheels for us?' 'Can a swim duck?' says Denny. 'Any particular colour?' When Denny was nine, he got his picture in the paper for nicking a double-decker bus, one of them real old-fashioned RTs with no synchromesh or nothing, like you only see in the Transport Museum nowadays. Got it nearly half a mile down the road before he hit the law car, and that was only because he was too short to see over the bonnet and double-declutch at the same time. So in about ten minutes flat Denny takes away and drives without the owner's consent a nice inconspicuous Cortina Mark 3 from four streets away and brings it down the bus stop where we're waiting for him. Spike tells him to drive it down towards Clapton and use the back doubles, but he still won't say exactly where we're going or why. Barry Crump says how about one point for every mod or punk we can make jump for it, two if we hit them and double points for niggers, but Spike says not, spoil the whole thing if we get nicked before we even get there. 'There' turns out to be that big triangle of waste ground with railway lines on all three sides down the bottom end of the Walthamstow Marshes, where the line out of Liverpool Street divides just after it crosses the River Lea. Spike makes Denny drive right into the middle of the triangle and says we're leaving the motor there; even if it's reported missing, the Old Bill's never going to find it there before morning. Denny wants to nick the car radio but Spike says to leave it, we got work to do. 'Come on,' says Denny, 'we're skint, that's a handsome radio, few quid there,' but it's no use arguing with Spike when his mind's set on something, it's like trying to get money out of a bubble. 'Follow me,' says Spike. 'Someone up there likes us tonight. Have one of you lot been being a good boy on the quiet?' And he explains how, like by magic, what we needs to do the job just happens to be kept right next to the ideal spot. All we got to do is break in and help ourselves. He's telling us all this while he's leading us along the towpath; it's a DIY warehouse we've got to get into, what we're after is paint. Under the railway bridge, Spike says 'Hoo Hoo' to test the echo over the water, then 'Abandon ship all ye who enter here!' 'Do what?' says Alf Rabaiotti. ' 'Morning, Alfred,' says Spike, and tips Alf into the Lea. That's where we discover Alf can't swim, due to being the one person in three million or whatever with negative buoyancy, and Spike and Barry have to go in after him to stop him drowning. Everyone's laughing fit to bust by the time they gets him out, and Spike has a hard time getting us to listen while he explains he's got the ideal spot for slogan-painting, right by the main line, millions of punters going past on the train every day, all we need is paint. 'Oh,' says Alf Rabaiotti, 'we going to do some painting?'

Well, Denny's in and out of the place in no time flat with jumbo aerosols for everybody, and we march out to where some factories and warehouses and things back on to the railway line. No worries about being seen from the trains; driver's watching the track, and you can't see nothing out a lighted coach when it's dark outside, can you? Anyway, Spike says Alf has to have the honour of painting up the first slogan, which surprises me, because when it comes to stringing words together, Alf Rabaiotti is generally about as much use as a chocolate teapot. And I can't work out whether Spike's taking the piss or whether he's trying to make old Alf feel good after looking such a berk in the river. 'Nice and big, now, Alf,' says Spike. 'They got to read it from the train,' and Alf steps up and paints ABANDON WOGS SLUM. And there's a bit of a pause, like, and then Spike says, 'Nice one,' and suddenly everyone's clapping Alf on the back and punching him on the arm and he's got this great big grin on his stupid face. It comes to me clear, then, something I've only sort of half-noticed before, that Spike's got some kind of magic way of making people do what he wants, and making them do it good. 'Last one to finish his spray-can's a wimp,' says Spike, and we spread out along the track painting away like we was nutty or something. Well, you'd be surprised how much wall-space five blokes can fill up when they're racing each other, and when we're finished it's too long to read it all from any one spot, and it looks really good. None of the individual bits is all that great, but there's so fucking *much* of it. I notice everybody, me included, seems to have used ABANDON WOGS SLUM at least once, and I can see where old Alf's brains give up on him and he's lapsed into SPURS SHIT CHELSEA SHIT. 'Ten points,' says Spike. 'Clear maximum.' Then we say goodnight and Spike goes off through the sidings to his place in the new estate on the other side of the line, and the rest of us come out through the playing-fields to see can we get a night bus back up here, due to Denny thinks two cars in one night might be pushing it.

And that's the last any of us ever saw of Spike. See, where

we'd been was the British Rail track with the overhead
electric, but them sidings is the marshalling-yard for London
Transport, the Tube trains, with the old live rail. And we'll
never know if old Spike slipped, or if he just plain forgot, but
he was still pretty soaked from being in the Lea, so when he
touched the live rail, *zap*.

Well, all the real devil seemed to go out of the lads after
that. We gradually sort of drifted apart, like, especially after I
got the driving job and the others are all still on the dole. Still
see them on the street to say hallo to and that, but we're going
around together less and less all the time. And though I've
always got all the memories of old Spike lying around somewhere at the bottom of my mind, it's been maybe a year or
more since I really thought much about any of it when I get
sent on this delivery job out to Stansted airport. So I makes
the drop, and I'm tooling along on my way home minding my
own business, when this stupid fucking wally in a Morris
Minor Traveller backs straight out of his weekend cottage
garden on a blind corner and *smash*. He's got Nuclear Power
No Thanks and Greenpeace and We Have Eaten The Lions of
Longleat stickers and all sorts of other shit all over his back
windows, so I don't reckon he could have seen me even if
he'd bothered to look. It's in absolutely perfect nick, or was
till I hit it, and you can tell it's his pride and joy and he's
probably even insured the no claims bonus and you know
before he even gets out that he's about thirty-five and bald
with baggy designer dungarees and a shoulder-bag. Oh what
a terrible shame, I thinks, now you won't be able to pavement-
park it in Camden Market (hey, that rhymes, maybe I could
get a song together on that, eh?). But it turns out he's really
nice about it, all his fault, sure you're OK, come in the house
and have a cuppa while he phones for the breakdown wagon,
because as well as killing the Morris, the smash has done my
Transit no good whatsoever. And when the recovery truck
geezer gets there, little fat smiley wop geezer, melon on legs,

no neck, gold tooth, oily black hair, he just bends down and squints under the front end and starts making these No Way wop gestures with his arms straight down, like he was ruffling the heads of two little kids. 'Ohohoho,' he says, 'Nononono,' he says, 'She ainta gonna fly no more,' he says, and I have to get the train back from Bishop's Stortford.

When I get on the train, there's these two oldish geezers sitting facing each other at the table opposite, and they both look away very quickly after giving me angry little stares that tell me they're thinking, Please, God, make the nasty rough skinhead lout not sit near us, God. And straight away they start to talk to each other just a little bit louder, as if that, and not looking at me, is somehow going to magic me away. And it's a really *smart* conversation, making me think they're college professors from Cambridge or something. '. . . and as far as I can make him out, Lodge appears to be arguing that the structuralist approach is valid because it enables him to ensure that mediocre undergraduates can hand up more substantial and coherent essays.' 'Ha. Crap, absolute crap. Tail-wagging-dog-ism.' But it don't bother me none, due to I've noticed when old people give you all them fierce frowns and that, it's really because they're frightened of you, not angry with you. So I just plonks my boots up on the seat opposite and gives this great big nutty smile which I know very well they can see out the corner of their eyes, and this makes them pretend even harder I'm not there. And they even start playing this college-professor game to keep the conversation from flagging '. . . you know the idea, the effects of the cuts are even spilling over into the titles of the stuff on the syllabus, Bleak Maisonette, Moderate Expectations, that sort of thing.' 'Ha ha. You could have, um, Submicroscopic Dorrit.' 'Ha ha ha.' And if the talk sounds a bit forced, you should hear the laughter. 'The Grapes of Pique.' 'Ha ha ha.' Funny how it's harder to make a meaningless noise like laughter sound real than it is to do the same with words.

'John Halifax, Estate Agent.' 'Ha ha ha ha ha.' Funny stuff, humour WELCOME TO WOGS SLUM Eh? What? FUCKING BLACK BARSTITS ABANDON TERRIBLE WOGS SLUM It's all there flashing past on the walls NIGGER BOY ANIMAL BURN WOG BABIES NOW But this ain't what we done, it's far too far north, way up near Brimsdown, miles away, we only done a hundred yards or so ON FIRE SAMBO ABANDON WOGS SLUM TERRIBLE TERRIBLE it's grown, it's enormous, someone's been adding to it and adding to it, it's like it's going on for ever SHITHOUSE COONS OUT NOW Jesus Christ, it's *huge*! And the *hate* coming off those walls, it's got me flinching in case it knocks the train off the rails KILL WOG SHIT ABANDON TERRIBLE WOGS SLUM and it's kind of frightening to think something a bunch of brainless kids done for a stunt can grow into something this big, and I'm wondering if poor old Spike ever realized he could start something this *scary*. And then I notice the professors is blind to it, still carrying on with their stupid game IF THEY'RE BLACK SEND THEM BACK 'The Antepenultimate Mohican.' 'Ha ha ha ha ha.' FUCKING BLACK BARSTITS 'Oh, wait, wait, I think this one's a boss. The Life and Opinions of Tristam Lemonade.' 'Ha ha ha ha ha.' TERRIBLE TERRIBLE ABANDON WOGS SLUM and then I suddenly twig that they know it's there, all right, they're regulars on the route, but they're ignoring it the exact same way they're ignoring me, because it scares the shit out of them and they don't want to see it. Them punters is well stunned, old Spike, I thinks, ten points, posthumous. SPURS SHIT CHELSEA SHIT ABANDON . . .

When we get past it all down by the Marshes, the poor old dead Cortina's still out there in the middle of the triangle of waste ground, and I'm wondering who got the radio.

Course, that's all ancient history now. Haven't seen any of the lads for ages. Heard Denny Plumb was in Brixton for breaking and entering, which don't surprise me, and someone was telling me the other day Barry Crump was getting married. Don't know what became of Alf Rabaiotti, but I bet he ain't married, probably still thinks what you do with girls is gob on their head off the top deck of a bus. And you can see I let my hair grow quite some time ago. What finally turned me, I seen this little kid about nine years old done out as a perfect miniature skin, haircut, boots, braces, the lot. Well, you can't go round looking like what a nine-year-old thinks is hard, can you? Anyway, chances are nowadays the next skin you will see will have a telly-producer dad in Parliament Hill Fields and think it's hard to write up shit like Tracey 4 Mark and Spliff + Snout in Finsbury Park and Camden Town and buy his boots in Kickself. I even seen one the other day with *green boots*.

But I was down that way again the other day, you know. Been down Petticoat Lane of a Sunday and decided to come home on the train for a change. And you know what? They cleaned it all off, wiped it out. The Council, or British Rail, or someone. Scrubbed it away, every word of it, painted over where they had to. Must have taken ages, cost a small fortune. But I'll tell you something really queer. It felt worse going past there if anything. I mean, you can easily see where the writing's been, and you can't help thinking about all them geezers having to clean up all them walls and things that the train takes ages to get past even at top speed. And that immediately reminds you of what it used to say, and that it wasn't just you, lots of other people felt so bad about it they went to all this trouble to wipe it out. And the laugh is, all they done was make it worse. Because I can see other people on the train who more than likely do the journey every day, they're feeling it even more than me. See, they got no excuse not to look out the window now, but when they do, the marks of the clean-up sets their minds going, don't they? The scrubbed wall shouts out all that hate louder than the wiped-out writing did. Really strange, by pretending something's never been said, you can end up screaming it. You learn something every day.

ABANDON . . .

MISTAKEN IDENTIFY

For Bill Morrison

When you come to a really big decision about the way your life is going, a decision that really matters, it very often casts your mind back right all along the whole way you have come so far, like the drowning man's life in the saying. That's what I've always found, speaking for myself. So when this business came up today, it wasn't any surprise to me when I found myself dwelling on all sorts of stuff I didn't realize I'd still remembered. What did surprise me was the thing that stood out as the high spot among all that memory. The mind was mainly on stuff connected with the job, of course, only to be expected in the circumstances. So what would you expect to be the strongest memory out of nearly twenty years as a London policeman? The Richardson case? Two Royal Weddings? The great Vietnam demo? The Spaghetti House siege? Even getting my picture in the paper as the Cheery Copper at the Notting Hill Carnival? Well, you'd be dead wrong. What stood out was Gurley Verity. Gurley bloody Verity, a half-arsed nobody of a dosser. Memory is a funny thing, and that's the plain truth.

I have been in the job for nineteen years come November, and this morning a young girl spat in my face, and this afternoon I wrote out my resignation. That is a thing I never ever thought I would do. At least, never until fairly recently. You see, this is – was – the only job I ever wanted to do. I had other jobs before, of course, but this is the only one I ever managed to really make a go of. It just seemed to come naturally to me, this job. It just somehow seemed to be what I was *for*. And I loved it, you know. I gave it everything I could. Oh, I grumbled about it with the best of them now and then, everybody does that, but underneath I still loved it. I've put in enough voluntary overtime in my day to make me the richest man in the graveyard twice over, and to bust up one marriage, and make the present one more than a bit lively at times, but I was *happy* to do it. I've never classed myself as any kind of thinker, and I did it all at the time without a second thought, but I've had chances enough over the years to puzzle things out, and what I've come to feel about it all is this: I loved the job because it *needed* me. It wasn't just that I loved doing something I thought I was good at, though that's bound to come into it; I really did think the job needed me. And you're always going to find it hard not to love something that needs you, aren't you?

But Gurley Verity, though. I can hear him now if I shut my eyes, that Scouse whine of his all mixed up with Cockney and Paddy and Yankee and BBC plus whatever else happened to take the old tow-rag's fancy. 'Ah, bless you Mr Purbeck, sare, pleasure to get locked up by a gentleman.' That would be on a cold night when he couldn't afford to get half as drunk as he was making himself out to be; a great actor, Gurley was. Is, I should say, he's still alive and kicking. More often than not, we'd take pity on him, even though we knew he'd stink the car out as bad as any other dosser with his three pairs of trousers he'd probably wet himself in every other night for God knows how long. 'Ah, you're a lovely driver, sare, this is me red nettle day tonight.' To this day, I am never really sure when Gurley mixes his words up whether he's doing it out of ignorance or drink or because it's his idea of a joke. He is one of the few people I've never really been able to read, a born performer. It's always been drink-related offences, of course, drunk and incapable, drunk and disorderly, breach of the peace, indecent nuisance. I don't think we ever got him for drunk in charge; as far as cars went, Gurley always seemed to be a confirmed passenger. But you never could tell what sort of performance you were going to get when you picked him up. 'You can't fool me,' he might say, 'you're not really there, it's the DTs, you're just a fitment of me imagination. Take me to the Polytechnic Hospital and hang me out to dry!' Or it might be, 'We know where you live, Purbeck! One finger on me and you can kiss yourself goodnight. And if you're going down any dark alleys, wear your second-best legs!' Or again, 'Philistines! *Hoodligans*! You're not fit to *speak* to a man of my calibre. Every one of youse is as thick as thieves!' I think making his whole life into a performance was the only way Gurley managed to cope with it. And I always had the feeling that the performance wasn't really for our benefit; he was his own audience. It was as though he only felt safe if he could believe that he was writing the script and, I don't know, somehow *directing* the rest of us as if we were bit players.

Once you got him to the station and the charge read out, though, the performance was always the same. 'Not signing nothing,' he'd say, 'I prefer to remain anomalous.' And, 'Look at them hands, sare. Haven't I got lovely hands?' (Ugly, fat and purple-red, just like his face.) 'Me mother used to say, them is the delicate hands of a brain pianist, or a concert surgeon.' When he was turning out his pockets, he always said, 'Count me money real careful, sare, and me miscellarious effects. Count them so they'll stay counted. I like me things to stay counted.' And every time in the magistrates' court, he gave the same speech from the dock. 'Never done nothing, sare. Innocent as the new-born snow. They got the wrong man. Clear case of mistaken identify.'

Over the years you get to hear quite a bit of business gossip from other Divisions, and I don't think there can be many nicks within five miles of Charing Cross that don't have at least one Gurley Verity story to tell. Some of the stories I've heard are almost too good to be true, like the one, West End Central I think, where the duty sergeant tells the constable to put Gurley in number eight. And Gurley's doing his Distressed Old Gentleman act, and on the way through he says, 'I say, old chap, what was that the sergeant was saying to you, getting a bit Mutt and Jeff, don't you know?' 'He was telling me to put you in number eight. The cell number.' '?' says Gurley, making with the deaf mime. And the lad bends down and bellows in Gurley's ear, 'You're in eight!' 'You taking the piss, sare?' says Gurley. So perhaps Gurley Verity is becoming almost a legendary sort of figure in his own way and it's not so surprising that he should stick out in my memory.

Legend or not, though, I did think when I started out that I'd have something more stirring to look back on at the end of my time than an old dosser. Oh, don't get me wrong, even when I started I didn't have any illusions about the job. I never thought I was going to be any glamour-boy hero hitting the headlines every other week with yet another breathtaking blow against organized crime or any nonsense like that. I'm a realist, always was. I know my own strengths and I know my own weaknesses. I knew all along that 90 per cent of the job was going to be routine and unexciting, boring even, but I accepted that. I knew I wasn't cut out to be the great detective, and I never even considered trying for CID. ('The CID, Mr Purbeck, sare,' Gurley Verity once said to me, 'the CID is uniformly corrupt.') And it pretty soon became plain to me that I wasn't cut out for promotion, either, but even that didn't bother me. You see, I'd worked out that the only thing I was really much above average at was people. You know, getting on with them quickly, seeing their point of view and getting them to see mine, that sort of thing. It seemed to me that staying on as a uniformed constable was the only way I could get to make the most of this and that is just what I have done. Oh, I dare say I could have got to sergeant or even inspector by now with average luck, but I think I've given more to the job and got more satisfaction out of it myself by doing things the way I have. I don't subscribe to the view that only a man trying to get promoted is going to do a really decent job. Most blokes aren't going to get promoted anyway, so if everybody's desperate for promotion you're going to find yourself with an awful lot of discontented coppers, and that can't be good for the job, now, can it?

Besides, I reckon it's better for the Young Bill to have a few old hands like myself out on the streets with them. I don't know if you've ever thought about it, but being a young policeman can be a very tricky proposition for the type of person you mostly get as a recruit. All their life, policemen have been sort of authority figures for them (the ones who get brought up to think of us as The Enemy tend not to join up), then suddenly, *wham*, they're It. And they find, surprise surprise, that doing your training at Hendon and putting on the uniform doesn't actually turn you into a wise and competent grown-up adult overnight, not even with all that Human Awareness and such they get nowadays. Instead, they suddenly realize why all their lives they've heard older people saying about how young the policemen are looking nowadays. It's because new policemen generally *are* young, and now they're It. Now a good sergeant can work wonders in guiding young chaps along the right lines in those circumstances, of course, but I maintain a seasoning of experienced mates in the ranks is a far better proposition. The nervous new boys are naturally going to be a bit backward about coming forward for help, and someone working alongside them is far better placed to see just when they need a tactful word of advice or encouragement and do the necessary. And the aggressive types with their balls still outgunning their brains, most of them are inclined to regard the sergeant as a bit of a challenge, and when they do need a firm telling-off – and nearly all of them do at some point – well, I've always found they'll take it far better from a mate who's not normally giving orders to them. I've always thought that side of my job was particularly important, and that's partly what I meant when I was talking just now about the job needing me.

I was talking about reading people a little earlier, too.

That's something I've always tried to get across to the Young Bill. I reckon there's no more valuable tool a policeman can have in his locker. It comes naturally to some but others have to be taught. That's why I say 'read', because it really is just like learning to read in school. You know, when you're little, and you have to keep on for ages going 'c-a-t, cat', then all of a sudden whole words start coming across at you off the page and you're away, reading. It's the same with the little individual details of expression and posture and movement and speech, suddenly you're reading *people*. Everyone does it a bit in their ordinary life, of course, but a policeman has got to be a professional at it. He's got to know what people are probably feeling and thinking, and more important at awkward moments, what they're likely to do next. Now as I say, I was always a natural at this, and in fact it was even a sort of hobby before I ever joined the force. So just recently when I seemed to be losing my touch at it, it naturally started me thinking about whether perhaps I'd really had enough of the job after all these years, and whether perhaps I shouldn't quit while I was still ahead.

I can remember the first time I noticed it. It was when I was taking Her Indoors out for a day at the Zoo. Animal daft, she is, loves the Zoo, but have you seen the prices recently? I don't know how they expect anyone with a family to afford it. We've no kids ourselves, of course. She can't, and we've never really thought seriously about adopting. Well, it wouldn't have made much sense with her being a nursing sister working shift hours nearly as daft as my own, would it? Anyway, as we were walking down from Camden Town Station, I was having my usual good old look around seeing what had changed since I was last that way, and spotting Irish accents. That's a game I made up when I was first there as a young copper more years ago than I care to remember. Now I expect you think all coppers are closet racists, but back then it was even more fashionable than nowadays to be strongly against anything like racial prejudice, and to believe that national characteristics were mostly noticed because that was what our bigoted elders had brought us up to expect to see. I was no exception to any of this, but while I was going through the business of learning to read people for myself, I couldn't help noticing how easy it was to spot the Irish by sight before you'd heard them speak. There's nothing to the game; you just pick yourself a distant face at random and quickly make it a mental No or Yes (Don't Know isn't allowed), then you put yourself where you can hear the accent and award yourself points accordingly. I reckon to score better than eight out of ten on the Yeses and not much worse on the Noes. Well, I'd never ever mentioned this game to Her Indoors, maybe because she's half Irish herself, and pretty soon she's starting to look a bit sideways at me. Finally she asks me what the hell I'm playing at and I have to explain it all to her. And she simply won't believe what I say about how high I score. 'Right,' I tell her, 'watch this.' By this time we've come to the top of Parkway, to that bit where the Euston line goes through a short tunnel under the road intersection. We're about thirty yards from a pair of black-painted wrought-iron public benches, the kind divided up by arm-rests into individual seats. Now it's a funny thing, but in all the times over the years I've passed those two benches, whatever the weather or the time of day, there's always been two or three drunks sitting on them, and this time is no exception. 'Those two on the bench', I tell Her Indoors, 'are definite Yeses, and I'll pay for your next hairdo if I'm wrong.' And they really do look a pair of racing certainties. One's the big agricultural spuds-and-shtout type, old pork-pie hat jammed down hard and square, mopping his dirty red face with a dirty red hanky; his mate is the foxy jockey sort, ginger hair going thin, swigging out of a quart cider bottle. So we walk past them slowly, pretending to look elsewhere, and at first it looks as though they're going to foil us by not speaking. Then they both sort of jerk out of their daydreams for no apparent reason. 'Whereof we cannot speak,' says Spuds-and-Shtout in a plummy BBC voice, 'thereof we must remain silent.' 'Fucking A,' says Foxy Jockey, pride of the Panhandle. Twenty quid, that cost me.

Not long after that, I was waiting for a bus near King's Cross station one rest Sunday. I don't run a car of my own, you know. I get all the driving I need and more at work, and in any case you can't really *do* anything else if you're driving. Read, I mean, or study strangers, or sleep. To me, driving is a complete waste of time. Anyway, there was this young West Indian girl already at the bus stop when I got there. She was all dressed up in her Sunday best, and I remember looking at my watch to try and work out whether she was coming from or going to church. I expect you've noticed how the immigrant communities still go in for the really old-fashioned dressed-up *respectable* type of church-going, the type our parents' generation were just starting to drift away from when I was growing up. I'm not particularly religious myself, but I have to admit I do like to see that sort of thing still going on. It's nice to see a young girl dressed up prettily without looking tarty or freaky. There was a young black boy walked past and he was dressed up too in the same way that has Sunday Service written all over it, nice dark suit, white shirt and everything. The girl spoke to him as he passed, and he smiled at her and muttered something polite-sounding without stopping. I was just thinking that our job would be a lot easier if all young people were so well brought up, when the girl turned around and looked up at me. 'You want business?' she asked. How wrong can you get?

There have been a couple of other cases recently where I have got this sort of thing completely wrong and it was beginning to raise questions in my mind about maybe being in the job too long. Oh, nothing like bad enough to jack it in just on that account, but the seed of the idea was planted.

I have known Tommy Bolt ever since we trained together, and we have never failed to get on famously whenever the job has thrown us together over the years. A lot of blokes don't like working with Tommy, because he isn't a chatty sort of bloke plus he can be a bit short when he's telling the younger ones when they're out of order, but he is definitely my sort of policeman. He keeps his head; all the time he's *thinking* away there, spotting trouble before it gets round to happening, doing the right thing to stop it happening, knowing what the right thing to do is. A lot of it's experience, of course, but to me, Tommy is a real natural. And when he does say something, it's nearly always something worth saying. That's more than you can say about most of the blokes who bitch about him being an unsociable old sod. 'I'm not sure I like your attitude,' this I Know the Commissioner Personally drunk driver once said to Tommy Bolt. 'Ah,' Tommy says, 'uncertainty everywhere these days, Sir. Blow in the bag, please.' And the drunk was so busy trying to work it out he blew as meek as a lamb. And another time, me and Tommy were going off duty together – where we were then, I used to go one way on the tube and he went the opposite, but we usually walked down together for a smoke and a chat until whoever's train came first. The long escalator was worse than ever, stuff all over it, URBAN STAB YOUTH SKANK POSSE LESBIANS IGNITE CLOCK END, I'm sure you've seen it yourself. But what particularly caught my eye on this occasion was the small advertisements by the moving handrail. Have you noticed they're not behind glass any more? Good thing, too, some idiot or other was forever smashing the panes to watch the broken glass slide down to the bottom. But it does mean that any twerp with a marker pen can scribble all over that exposed glossy plasticky stuff the ads are printed on. And every single ad on our side had SHARON WOZ ERE OR BOOPO + DONKER or some such on it, every single one. Marvellous thing, education, isn't it? I pointed this out to Tommy Bolt as we were going down. He didn't say anything at first, just kept staring at the ads and chewing his gum. A great chewer of gum, old Tommy. But when we got to the bottom, he turned to me and said straight-faced, 'Some people,' he says, 'some people never read anything without signing it first.'

Anyway, one thing Tommy said to me a few years ago now has always stuck in my mind. It was when we were doing a Christmas Day turn together. We were just motoring around to pass the time away, really, neither of us felt like a nap, even though there was absolutely nothing doing to keep awake for. Have you ever driven around these parts just after daylight on Christmas morning? If you know the roads well enough, you can safely drive blindfold, for you'll not see a pedestrian or another vehicle for half an hour at a stretch. Now normally the thing that strikes people about Tommy Bolt is his self-control. Never loses his rag, whatever the provocation, stays ice-cool, absolutely correct. Some wag once suggested that when things really did get too much for Tommy, he went off by himself down the bottom of his garden and dropped Tupperware on to foam-rubber cushions until he felt better. But on this day I reckon Tommy must have been feeling the Christmas spirit or something, because when we came to that big roundabout by the flyover, he just kept driving round and round it whistling 'Here We Go Round The Mulberry Bush', going faster and faster until he was just below the speed where the tyres would have started to squeal. I kept reading all the five sets of exit signs as they went past again and again, both the local London district names and the feeder routes for the trunk roads out of town. It struck me how there was an awful lot of really complicated planning went into something like that, working out the best compromise of which ways to send all the various chunks of peak traffic with the minimum snarl-ups. Thinking about stuff like that normally gives me the willies. Thinking about a simple kid's jigsaw puzzle too hard gives me the willies. But it caught my fancy on this occasion and I said something about it to Tommy, and about how great the exit signs were and how it was impossible to go wrong because if you weren't sure you could always go round another time for a more careful look. Tommy stopped whistling and started chewing and took his foot off the accelerator. And then, with no word of warning – *wheeeeeee*. .! – he's swung us right round and there we are going round the mulberry bush the wrong way. 'Read me a single sign,' says Tommy, 'see, the signs are all unreadable if you start off pointing in the completely wrong direction.'

Now I don't think Tommy was being – is it 'metaphorical' I'm trying to say or 'metaphysical'? Never could remember the difference. But whether Tommy meant it or not, what he said isn't a half bad way of describing how so many of the youngsters that pass through our hands just get stuck on the rails the wrong way round. It's like they start out facing away from the signs, for whatever reason, and very likely the first sign they actually get is something nasty going the other way smashing into them. And either that does them a serious hurt, or it makes them start fighting against people who are actually the ones going the proper way. In either case, they very likely never get to learn to read the signs. They finish up, maybe for life, like the friendly dog that thinks the angry cat's wagging tail means pussy's pleased to see him. I took a lot of stick from blokes at work for talk like that over the years, you know. Get him, bleeding-heart liberal social worker, *Grauniad*-reading wimp and so on and so forth, I expect you know the kind of thing. It's not surprising given the sort of blokes we mostly manage to recruit as policemen, though I must say the better money nowadays does seem to be changing that. I'm not running them down, the traditional sort of recruits, mind. I really do think most of them are the salt of the earth and I don't care if you do think that sounds corny. But I have to admit that most of them do like to see things as simple issues

161

of black and white, right and wrong, cops and robbers if you like. Because that makes life easier for them, of course, removes any doubts they might have about who they are or what they're doing. Well, nobody enjoys doubts, do they? But for all the wisecracks, I still hold to that belief. I keep telling the younger ones, if you want to believe that complicated stuff like that is really simple, go ahead and good luck to you, but as far as reading people is concerned you will stay a bunch of illiterates. I stick to my own ideas. Plus I have always been a *Mail* reader.

Now there are times in police work where that sort of fancy theorizing has no practical place at all. I am the first to admit that. When some young cowboy has drunk himself brainless and is measuring you up for a kick in the cobblers, it makes far better sense to concentrate on keeping your hip turned towards him than to start trying to strike up a meaningful social relationship. And when two or three hundred teenage football fans have got enough alcohol and adrenalin into their veins to turn a bunch of neighbourhood kids into a potentially lethal mob, any commendations you get for appealing to their better natures are likely to be posthumous. And riots – riots are generally made up of ordinary decent people who have gone several steps backwards towards being completely animal. Temporarily insane, if you like. The old thing in the history books about reading the riot act to mobs, that always did make me laugh. If a crowd really has gone past the point of becoming a mob, you might as well read them *Roy of the Rovers*. Reading the riot act could never have done any good at all, except maybe salving the conscience of the poor bloody squaddies who got the orders to shoot.

The riots round here have already become a part of local folklore. Funny, really, it only seems like the day before yesterday, doesn't it? But when you drive down on the main road from Stockwell where the Council have done all that Lambeth Welcomes You to Brixton clean-up stuff, there's a big traffic sign reading BRIXTON SHOPS OPEN AND COVERED MARKETS CIVIC AMENITIES *RIOTS*, the last hand-aerosoled, of course. It doesn't seem to matter how often they clean it off, *RIOTS* comes right back overnight. *RIOT* say the hand-painted slogans on the walls along Gresham Road and Coldharbour Lane and Effra Road, even as far away as the Elephant, *RIOT*. Nobody does, of course. It's just a nice dramatic word that appeals to the kids who like making a bit of a splash. *RIOT* doesn't actually mean any more than OI! A NUT or DEN BOOT GIRLS or JIMMY THE HOOVER. But the actual riots, they were real enough and I've got the scars to prove it. Don't worry, I'm not going to bend your ear on that subject. I'm sure you've already had quite enough about that on the telly and in the papers at the time, not to mention the public enquiry the politicos felt obliged to hold afterwards to prove to themselves they really do have some effect on the lives of ordinary people like you and me. All I will say is this. I was there, and I was absolutely bloody appalled, but I went ahead and tried to do my job as best I could. That kind of thing I have always looked on as just another part of the job. It's one of the things policemen are *for*. You can't expect any job to be all a bed of roses in my view, and police work is certainly no exception.

So I had no complaints, and no more did Tommy Bolt who had far more reason to complain, having got himself kneed in the cobblers by some berserk teenager on a kamikaze charge against Babylon, and then having the same kid's parents bring a private prosecution against him for assault and malicious arrest. Tommy got off, of course, but he took it all without complaint or show of ill-feeling, which is the kind of thing I meant when I said he was my sort of policeman. A lot of the blokes were very bitter after those riots, and especially over how some of the media kept making out it was the police to blame and that we somehow dropped off by letting it all happen in the first place. Well, that is a pretty dog-brained sort of notion. If you read in the history books, you will see there have been mobs and riots as long as there have been cities. I doubt if any real city anywhere has ever gone a hundred years without something that could be classed as a riot of sorts. It's the other side of the coin, you could say. You get a community big enough to give you all the energy and variety of real big-city life, and you seem to automatically get the potential for a mob to form, too. The actual excuse can be anything, religion, politics, race, food taboos, anything may be enough to set it off. You can't blame anyone for that, in my view. You might almost say you can define a city as a town big enough to produce its own mob in the right combination of circumstances, and what's London but half a dozen or more towns like that all run together?

But you're letting me ramble on here; the real point I wanted to make to you is that I can understand those blokes who felt bad about the stories without really agreeing with them. I think it is a bit naive to expect balanced media coverage of that sort of thing. The press boys are always going to write what they think their readers want to read. And some of them don't have a very high opinion of their own readers in that respect, do they? I don't just mean the tabloids, mind, the highbrow papers are just as bad even if they do use more big words, but I think you just have to accept that as inevitable. I mean, who's going to write Two Hours of Confused Scuffling and Shouting, Some Injuries to Police and Public when he thinks his readers would rather see Black Terror Mob Runs Amok or Community Leaders Condemn Police Aggression? Even when we have to do an official report of an incident for possible use in evidence, it's never exactly everything as it happened, you have to pick and choose the relevant bits and put them in some sort of order. Someone who reads what someone else has written about an incident is never, except by a fluke, going to learn exactly what that incident was like in practice. I don't know why they can't teach that to kids in school a lot better than they do.

This morning, Tommy Bolt was right on the top of his form. I was just putting my paper on the shelf above the dash when he got into the passenger seat, and he jabbed a finger at the headline I'd left exposed: MY LUCK, BY CAR RAPIST. 'If he rapes cars,' says Tommy, 'he's lucky to still have a dong.' Coming round by the big church, there was the usual small sort of demo standing there, dozen or two people, perfectly peaceable, with a banner saying ALL MEN ARE BROTHERS. 'Ever know any brothers that didn't fight?' Tommy says to me. We were having one of those really super shifts when you're both of you in a good mood and so's Joe Public, even the waifs and strays. There was hardly anything for us to do bar give directions to strangers, and even the one old dear I thought we might have to get the mental welfare to, even she turned out to just want someone in authority to listen to her for ten minutes. Tommy handled her beautiful, too. 'Yes, madam, terrible,' he says, nodding away all solemn, 'you're very brave to put up with it, too,' and her rambling on about the burglars and the neighbours and drug addicts and Irish and the price of pink paraffin, 'Yes, you're so right – getting this all down, I hope, George? It's very good of you to be so public-spirited as to keep us informed. Rely on us. We shall put a stop to all of it. Thank you,' and off she goes as pleased as punch. A great day, we were having.

And then it happened. It was Tommy who noticed them first; left to myself and I might have driven straight past, being sort of lulled by the good times we'd been having all morning. 'Pull over smart and call in for a WPC!' he says, and off out the passenger door almost before I'd stopped. He made a bee-line for them while I was still on the radio, and I saw straight away what he meant. The two of them were on the wide pavement just along from the old town hall, and it was as if they were in a kind of clearing all of their own with all the passers-by giving them a wide berth and hurrying on their way. The heads were all turning as they went by, but nobody was stopping to watch and listen. You got the idea that one brief passing glimpse was enough to convince them that what was going on was unpredictable and maybe dangerous, rather than interesting or funny enough to stop and gawp at. That's what Tommy had been so quick to spot, I expect.

They were both black and I mentally put them down straight away as mother and daughter. I don't know why, there was no real family-type resemblance as far as I could see. Perhaps it was something in the younger one's attitude to the other. Plus the age difference, of course. The older one, the one doing all the shouting and bawling, she was about forty, a big wide stocky woman to start with and badly overweight, quite well-dressed – not Sunday Best, maybe, but definitely several cuts above Housework. The younger one – well, the older I get, the harder I find it to judge their ages, the teenagers, but she was certainly fifteen and maybe even twenty. She was a tall awkward skinny girl, the kind that has trouble knowing where to put their hands and feet when they're standing still, but what struck you more was the way her whole head and body, no matter which way she moved, seemed to be fixed into one big permanent flinch. The kind of thing you see quite often in a battered toddler, only this was a seemingly healthy young grown-up woman. Anyway, it turned out after it was all over that I'd been right. They were mother and daughter.

I was still seeing all this from inside the car at that stage, with the windows shut to keep down the traffic noise on the radio, so I couldn't actually hear what was going on on the pavement. I could see all right, though. The mother was screaming and shouting fit to bust at the daughter, swaying back and forth from the waist, or where the waist would've been if she'd still had one, giving it all she'd got. She had an old-fashioned leather handbag clamped high under her left armpit, and she kept pounding the handbag with her right fist to emphasize whatever it was she was saying. Or yelling, more like. The daughter wasn't saying a thing. She was just standing there, shuffling, fidgeting, looking steadily at her own shoes, a long beanpole of a girl a good head taller than her mother. Every so often she made a most peculiar little movement, almost like a tic. She would suddenly sort of swoop and half-turn away from her mother, lifting her face up as if she wanted to appeal to someone passing, but then she always snapped back round like she was on elastic or something to face her mother again. Every time this happened, the mother seemed to get driven even more frantic, screaming and punching away at her handbag nineteen to the dozen until her daughter's eyes were beaten back down to the floor. Tommy had come up to them by this time and was doing his level best to calm things down, without much success. The mother more or less ignored him. The daughter never so much as looked at him. Every time Tommy tried to put himself between the pair of them, the mother just circled a wide step to her right, shoved the elbow with the handbag under it past Tommy's side, stepped forward and banged him out of the way with a sideways thump of the hips. She must have had two stone on him, and he stood no real chance if he wanted to avoid getting really physical and maybe doing her some damage. She hardly seemed to slacken the screaming and bawling while she was barging him aside, either.

Then I was out of the car and over to give Tommy a hand, and for the first time I could actually hear the mother, but I was none the wiser for that. She was easy enough to hear, because the voice was even more powerful than you might have expected from the look of her, but she was well-nigh impossible to understand. I think it was mostly in one of those French-based patois lingos that some of the West Indian people speak amongst theirselves, but to be quite honest it might as well have been Ancient Greek for all Tommy or I could make of it. There was no mistaking the tone, though, even if we hadn't been able to see how the girl was taking it. That mother was angry, and full up to bursting with shame and frustration and disappointment and maybe a few other things I don't have the words for, and most definitely out of control, totally. By the time I got right up to them, she'd changed her tactics from just bumping Tommy out of the way. Every so often, she was now suddenly breaking off the patois shouting and spinning round to give Tommy a quick burst of the verbals in finest Brixton English, 'Mind you bloody business! Why you not let a person be?' and then straight back in on the daughter. And when I got there, of course, she immediately started giving me the same treatment. 'Shame, shame!' she screams at me, 'You leave we be! You leave we be and go catch tiefs!' and straight back in on the poor girl *again*.

Now that there were two big strong uniformed coppers on the spot to protect them, passers-by were starting to linger and gape, so that as well as trying to calm the mother down, Tommy and I had to try and keep the crowd moving at the same time. The last thing you want when you're trying to calm down an incident like that is a crowd of spectators. Either you start getting secondary outbreaks between supporters of the quarrelling parties, or the whole crowd swings in favour of the one side and turns nasty, and if you think it's Old Bill's side the whole crowd swings to, you can go and stand in the corner till playtime. The mother didn't seem too worried over whether she collected an audience or not, but she was getting more and more desperate in her attempts to drive off Tommy and me, so much so that she was sometimes forgetting to switch back to patois when she rounded on the girl, not that that seemed to make much difference. I was beginning to wonder whether we mightn't calm her down better by pulling back for a bit. I was thinking of suggesting as much to Tommy; I'd got a bit separated from him through having to escort a couple of early lunchtime drunks away from the free show. Then I heard the mother break off from giving Tommy a proper roasting and scream at the girl, 'Shame bitch, you go *stab up!*, and suddenly there was this great big ugly knife in her right hand; she whipped it out of that old black handbag and went straight at the girl, shrieking, no words.

And do you know, that girl *did not move*. She stood there in that same long flinch, head down, looking up out of the corners of her eyes at the knife, *waiting for the knife*. It was like she knew she'd only get worse if she tried to dodge it.

Tommy moved, all right. In all the years I've known him, I never saw him move so fast. He had the woman's arm up behind her back and the knife on the deck before you could say, well, 'Knife'. He was a bit leery of her from the buffeting she'd given him earlier, though, and he was bellowing loud and clear for assistance from yours truly, which was already on the way, of course. But it wasn't needed. The fight had all gone out of her and she was in floods of tears. No more shouting, she just wept and wept and seemed quite indifferent when Tommy started to lead her away to put a safe distance between her and the daughter. I went to make sure the girl was OK but it was hard to tell. She wasn't speaking, and I couldn't really be sure I was getting through to her at all. She wouldn't look at me; she was still counting her feet most of the time and rocking slightly from side to side. When she did this, I noticed she kept trying to see past me first on one side then the other, though still with her head hung down, looking out of the corner of her eye. Then I got it – she was trying to look at her mother. And I stood aside and let her, and it was clear to me there was more to it than just looking. She still wasn't saying anything, but she didn't need to. She wanted to go with her mother. After *that*, all she seemed to be worried about was going with her mother, *but she couldn't leave the spot where she stood without her mother's permission*. The further away Tommy took her mother, the more distressed the girl got, until she was actually whimpering out loud and making little jerky half-waves with her hands and jiggling on the spot, a bit like a young kid trying to attract teacher's attention to leave the room. I looked at that girl, and I had one of those sort of *flashes* you can sometimes get, you know, when you suddenly know plain as plain *exactly* what the other person is feeling? I *knew* what that girl was feeling.

And it was bloody *awful*, you know?

Well, then the car with the WPC arrived, plus two wide-awake traffic boys on motor bikes spotted our uniforms and stopped to assist with the crowd, and it seemed it was all over bar the paperwork. Did I tell you that on top of everything else, Tommy Bolt is an absolute demon for paperwork? Can't abide it, myself. Can't avoid it in police work, either, more's the pity. Many's the time I've thought that if I were a tree I'd take out a contract on whoever it was laid down our paperwork system; the Met alone must go through a forest a fortnight in paper. But old Tommy loves it, eats it up. Anyway, it turned out he'd left his notebook in the car, so off he toddled to fetch it. I expect he was secretly feeling a bit pleased with himself, coming out of an incident like that with his skin in one piece, though Tommy would never let anything like that show. He definitely couldn't have been himself one way or another, because the real Tommy Bolt would never in a hundred years have opened the offside door without checking the wing-mirror and stepped right into the path of a milk-float. That's right, a milk-float. Imagine surviving a mad heavyweight knifewoman only to get creamed by a *milk-float*. It was only doing about ten, of course, but it still knocked him flying into the open car door so that he went down very awkwardly, and the rear wheel crushed both his legs below the knee before poor old milko knew what was happening.

The worst part of it was, poor old Tommy never lost consciousness, not even for a second. We did our best to make him comfortable, but first aid can't do an awful lot for a bloke with injuries like that. He never made a sound, but that was the old Tommy Bolt control back in charge. I think he knew if he let himself use his voice at all it would be bound to come out as a scream. He kept looking at us and shaking his head, then closing his eyes, then opening them and shaking his head again. He had an expression on his face like someone who's agreed to give up the deeds to the ranch then been told they're going to get sawn in half anyway, just for the hell of it, and the five minutes we spent waiting for the ambulance were the longest five minutes of my life.

When we'd finally sent old Tommy off safely to hospital, I set myself to get stuck in and clear up all the loose ends of the original incident with the two women. I expect you might think that a callous sort of thing to do, you know, with your best mate just having maybe got himself crippled for life, just to go on with your job like that. But I've learnt over the years that it's the only way to cope with the really bad stuff that you're bound to get every so often. Keep busy, keep functioning as a professional, don't stop and brood. As long as you can keep yourself going like that you'd be surprised what you can get through, and you're a lot better in yourself for it as well as a lot more use to everyone else. Well, the WPC had persuaded the mother to sit in the back of her car, and she seemed to have quietened down to the point of going into some sort of trance. The daughter was a different kettle of fish, though. Would you believe that girl was *still* rooted to the spot where I'd left her? The WPC was doing her best, but she was making no impression whatsoever, so I went over to assist. I thought I had the answer, see, I thought I had it all worked out how to get through to the daughter. I tipped the WPC the wink to move aside, and I put on my best professional smiling fatherly manner, and I told the girl it was all right, her mother said it was all right for her to come with us to the car, and then maybe we'd all go for a nice drive together. Do you know, I really thought for a moment I'd cracked it? Her eyes lit up a bit, and she gave a shy sort of half-smile, and I was sure I'd cracked it. But then she pulled one of her swoop-about-face-and-whip-back numbers, and as a finishing touch she spat full in my face and slumped back as dead and sullen as ever.

I walked away smartish to keep my temper from breaking, but all the same something sort of snapped inside and I thought to myself, George, you most definitely do not bloody well need stuff like this. And when I came off duty at lunchtime, the first thing I did was to write out my resignation from the force, right there in the locker-room.

I didn't say anything to anybody at the time; they were mostly far more concerned with finding out from the hospital how Tommy Bolt was getting on, and arranging for someone to break the news to Tommy's wife. I had no appetite for lunch, and I didn't particularly feel like going home to sit by myself indoors, Mary being on days this week, so I ended up going for a long walk. I've always liked walking, I find it sort of comforting. In the finish, I probably put in four or five miles this afternoon, including going all the way round Brockwell Park a couple of times. And it was during this walk that I was going over all the old memories of the job that I was speaking about earlier on. I'd no doubts about what I'd done, you understand. I was maybe a bit worried over how I was going to explain myself to Mary, but I had no doubts at all that I was doing the right thing. Do you know, I don't think I'd even considered what I was going to do with the rest of my life, I was that sure I was making the right decision. Anyway, eventually it was starting to get dark and I set out for the tube to go home. I thought of getting the bus outside the park, but then I decided to walk along Railton Road, the whole length of it from Herne Hill station up to Market Row, to sort of say goodbye to it, I suppose. Hardly the sort of place I'd be visiting much in future, you might say. Well, the weather was turning pretty dismal by this time, and there's never very many people out and about at that hour of a Sunday afternoon, but even so, I couldn't help thinking that it wasn't nearly as depressing as you might expect it to be. Oh, there's still some shops boarded up or with heavy-duty grilles, but there's also quite a bit of rebuilding and refurbishment work newly finished or still going on. I'm sure you could quite easily find me more depressing streets in Wandsworth or Willesden or Bow or Bermondsey if you wanted to, and I've certainly walked down worse streets in my time than Railton Road.

And then they appeared. One minute there was nobody at all in sight, the next they sort of erupted into the street in a burst of shouting and laughter and blaring music from a ghetto-blaster cassette thing that one of them was carrying, out of a door about twenty yards behind me. Three of them, tall athletic-looking young chaps in windcheaters and Rasta caps, all as black as your hat. They went dead quiet for a moment when they saw me, except for the thump and crash and squawk from the tape-box, then they put their heads together and spoke quietly for a space before turning to walk along the pavement behind me. They kept their distance and stayed fairly quiet most of the time apart from the music, but every so often one or other of them would give a shout of laughter or a high-pitched giggle. Whenever I glanced back at them, they would meet my eye for a second with funny *knowing* smirks on their faces, then they would drop their heads, looking as if they were having a lot of trouble keeping their faces straight. Now at first I told myself not to be imagining things without cause, that people who go along expecting trouble very often attract it or even provoke it. But I couldn't help thinking at the same time that there was nothing to be lost by being careful, so, very gingerly I might add, I began to test out whether they really were tailing me. I slowed down to a stroll. They slowed down too and kept more or less the same distance between us. I speeded up a bit.

So did they. I stopped and looked in a shop window. They stopped and dawdled too. I crossed over to the other pavement. So did two of them; the one with the ghetto-blaster stayed on the same side – both pavements covered. No doubt about it, I had company. Now as you can tell by looking, I'll not see forty again and I could do with being a stone or more lighter, and even as a young man I was never exactly a sprinter, so there was no chance in making a break for it, they'd have gobbled me up inside thirty yards. And while I can use myself in a tight corner as well as the next bloke, I couldn't really rate my chances very high against three big strong boys with maybe twenty years' start on me. George, I said to myself, it looks like you are going to get your lumps. Just then one of them shouted, 'Hey!' and they turned off the music. I didn't look round; I was concentrating on walking as fast as I could without breaking into a run, trying to get as quickly as possible to where there might be some assistance. There was nobody else in sight, absolutely deserted. All I could hear was these three sets of footsteps going faster and faster to keep up with me and, yes, gaining on me – I could hear their breath now, all three of them were panting a bit. I was panting more than a bit myself, and desperately trying to remember what I should be doing to protect myself when they got me down, how best to fall and cover up and so on, and I was horrified to find my mind had gone a complete blank. The footsteps were very loud now, and the voice that had shouted before now broke into a queer high wordless yipping, then there was a sudden clatter of running, harsh and angry-sounding, and I whipped around to face – nothing.

That's right, nothing, a completely empty street. I stood there, out of breath, heart pounding, firmly convinced I had finally gone round the twist. Then I noticed the lighted doorway, four or five buildings back. They must have ducked in there for some reason. Every other door in sight was tight-shut and there was no cover at all to hide them. When I'd got my breath back and stopped shaking, more or less, I moved carefully back on the opposite side of the street until I could see into that doorway. Sure enough, my three lads passed across it one after the other, carrying stacks of chairs through an inner door. Then I read the signboard.

Pentecostal Mission Church.

The trouble with coincidence, Tommy Bolt has always been fond of saying, is that you can't rely on it, but when I'd finally more or less stopped feeling foolish and turned into Electric Avenue to come down to the tube, who was sat sheltering under the covered bit on an apple-box with a bottle of VP Rich Ruby for company? 'Is that yourself, Mr Purbeck, sare?' he says, 'only I can't see so good without me contract lenses.' Gurley Verity, of course. 'You're never going to lock us up on a lovely soft afternoon like this, Mr Purbeck?' I told him I wasn't in that line of work any more. 'Too sober to get locked up yet, honest. Say anything you want, go on, test me. *How now brown owl?*' He looked about as sober as closing time on election night, but you couldn't be sure with Gurley, him being so good an actor that he stays in character when he passes out. 'Join us in a farewell drink, Mr Purbeck. Bring on the dancing girls and break out the Green Chanteuse.' I told him I was on the waggon but he could have one for me. 'Ah, live for ever, Mr Purbeck!' he says, taking a great swig of hangover, 'live for ever, or – I'll *kill* youse!' And again, as I was coming away, he called to me, or maybe he was just rehearsing his speech in the dock for the 10,000th time, 'Never done nothing, sare! Mistaken identify . . . !'

I have been a London policeman for nineteen years come November, and this morning a young girl spat in my face, and this afternoon I wrote out my resignation. And just before I came in here tonight, I tore it up and stuffed it in the bin.

THE FASCINATION OF THE VANITY

For Susan Jeffreys

In school I was always The Poet's Daughter. Father's smallish name was made quite young. Miss Darnell was determined to make aesthetes of us, poor thing, and took great delight in exposing my secret at an early date. The dormitory Mafia tended towards hearty philistinism in the lower years and I feared nocturnal teasing, but they held off. By the time we reached the Fifth, Father had actually started to gain me kudos. I didn't really want to be The Poet's Daughter, of course. You always want what you haven't got. I wanted to walk on my hands and sit a horse and win at tennis like Wendy Pyecroft, but nobody my shape ever walked on her hands. But it did this much for me: by the time I left I'd been The Poet's Daughter so long that I was quite determined to be Me from then on.

I bumped into Wendy Pyecroft last year, thirty-odd years on. She looked awful. Breakdown. Just spent six months in Friern Barnet, poor girl. And the shrinks had told her that part of the trouble was her lack of a strong father-figure.

We buried Father last week. A dry old stick, you would have said, had you been acquainted. Eighty-four, and a widower for forty-one years. Jane – she's the younger daughter, two years younger than I am – she kept house for him all her life. A sort of life imprisonment, you might say. (Is life imprisonment a cruel and unnatural punishment? Is any punishment natural and uncruel?) Jane looks well enough on it. She's kept her looks and health far better than I have.

But we were speaking of Father. A wonderful old gentleman, they would any of them tell you in the street. So dignified. Such a lovely smile for everybody. Marvellous for his age.

179

Such a treat to see someone come so completely to terms with the limitations imposed on him by time, serene, not bitter. And so reliable, you could set your watch by him. There's not many round here you'd feel easy talking about that way; they're a decent enough crowd, but stand-offish. It's always been part of the price you pay for living in a good area of London. Not that a lot of them would concede that Kew is really 'London'. But I wonder what they'd say if they knew the real truth about Father.

For over forty years, he took the same walk every day. He used to cut through to the South Circular, the Mortlake Road bit, and then turn left and walk along to Kew Green. I'd have stuck to the side streets myself, far better to walk a bit farther and keep away from the traffic noise, but you could never get Father to listen to reason about anything like that. Then he used to buy a paper and some cigars, and sit on a bench on the Green for a bit. On rainy days, he took along yesterday's paper to sit on and his brolly to sit under. At precisely a quarter past eleven on weekdays, and at twelve on the dot every Sunday, you could've seen him walk into the Bold Princess Royal and order a small ruby port. He was convinced it was good for his blood, but he never had more than the one glass. They all knew him in the Princess, of course, but he hardly spoke to any of them. The bar staff didn't even know his name. He was always the kind of man people naturally call 'sir' even when he was still relatively young. He was back home again in time for Jane's lunch at two unless he'd given notice that he was lunching out. For years we thought he just dawdled round Kew Gardens after he left the pub. 'My constitutional,' he'd announce to Jane in the morning after he'd drunk his coffee, and that'd be him out of the house until two o'clock. It fairly floored both of us when we found out the truth, I can tell you.

He was seeing a woman. A widow, twelve years his junior, a Mrs Wilshire. She had a small house in Strand-on-the-

Green, just along from Oliver's Ait, and with that address I
don't need to tell you she must have been at least as well off
as Father. There was never any suggestion of anything mer-
cenary between them; it was purely an affair of – whatever it
was an affair of. He'd been seeing her every day for fifteen
years when Jane found out about it.

He never said a word to either of us on the subject, of
course. He'd done his level best to keep it completely secret
from everybody. He never walked there direct from the
Princess; he varied his route every day as though he were a
marked man. Some days he walked nearly half a mile out of
his way to Chiswick village and back. Other days he rode
around in a taxi for a quarter of an hour or more beforehand.
That's how Jane first saw him; he was getting out of a taxi
beside the Post Office in Thames Road. She was across there
visiting one of her old ladies. (I'm afraid Jane is much given
to lame duckery of all kinds. Just as well, I suppose. Had she
been different, we should've had to pay for a housekeeper for
Father all these years. There was never any suggestion of
marriage to Mrs Wilshire as far as we could tell.) Jane may be
a bit of a mouse, but she is a very nosy mouse. Her curiosity
got the better of her timidity with no difficulty whatsoever,
and she started to tail Father like someone in a cheap film.
She could have made a career as a tail, come to think of it. She
is the most inconspicuous person I know. Sitting in a room
with Jane can be very lonely. But to cut a long story short,
Father, for all his caution, had managed to get himself involved
with a woman whose next-door neighbour was another of
Jane's old ladies. It was actually quite surprising that Jane and
Father had managed to avoid bumping into each other on the
doorstep long before that.

A coincidence? I take the view that coincidences are no
more unlikely than any of the other possibilities. It was no
more and no less unlikely that Jane's old lady should live next
door to Mrs Wilshire than that she should live ten streets

181

away; it was simply more memorable, more noticeable. More remarkable, in the *other* sense of that word.

Jane didn't tell Father that she knew. Jane would sooner fall through the floor than bring such a thing up with Father. She told *me*, of course, and I should have had no qualms at all about bringing it up with him had there been any need to, but that was just it. There never was any need to. It was no trouble to us. Not another soul knew, apart from that next-door old lady of Jane's, and she didn't count. We just carried on as before. It was a good enough life we had, after all. We never wanted for a thing either of us could reasonably have hoped to get. Father denied us nothing provided the budget could stretch to it and it didn't disturb his own routine. His people had made an almost indecent pile in Africa so long ago that I doubt if we shall ever know exactly how, and Father was sole heir. And with my own salary on top – well, shall we just say that an Under-Secretary in Her Majesty's Civil Service is by no means as lowly or as impoverished as the title of the grade might suggest. We were happy with things as they were. Why make waves, as our American cousins say? So every morning, year in, year out, it was, 'My constitutional', and not so much as an eyebrow raised by Jane.

It's an old house we've got here – 1790s – with the original nine-foot brick wall around garden enough for a peacock, as Father always says. Said, I mean. Father was never a talkative man, but he had a true ear for the striking phrase. I like to think I've inherited it. I know I drive some of my staff wild by forever redrafting their efforts, but I simply refuse to sign anything unclear or inelegant. I regard it as a personal contribution to the battle against declining standards. Some of my Principals and Assistant Secs try to tell me that the battle was lost a generation or more ago, that nowadays one's fortunate to get correct spelling and grammar, never mind clarity or elegance. I refuse to give in to them. You don't get where I've got by giving in when you're in the right. I fully expect they'll be glad to see the back of me when I retire next year. I can't say I'll miss them overly, either. This last year or two I've increasingly begun to look on the office as an intolerable waste of garden time.

You'll notice I said 'garden', not 'gardening'. I do not garden. Jane gardens. As far as one can tell, Jane genuinely loves to garden, and would very likely be offended if anyone offered to assist her. I do not tend our peacock garden; I use it. I walk in it, sit and read in it, sleep in it, appreciate and love it. We do not, of course, keep a peacock in it. Nasty stupid noisy boorish birds. Our peacock garden is an island of quiet. Jane keeps her lawns looking positively edible, and there is a network of old paved paths that stay puddle-free even in downpours. Not crazy paving, exactly, but certainly slightly neurotic. We have shade on sunny days and shelter on windy ones, thanks to an old Black Italian Poplar and an even older Holm Oak. And, of course, to that lovely lovely wall. Our house is Listed, and we should have no end of trouble if we ever, God forbid, wanted to lower our nine-foot beauty. Most of our neighbours would dearly love our privacy, but the same planning committee that forbids us to touch our wall consistently refuses them planning permission for anything over five feet high. Why do I find such petty idiocies so deeply heartening?

There was a time when I used to find them infuriating, especially when forced to participate in them at work. Not that I was ever, thank heaven, involved in planning permission, but every aspect of public administration throws up its own idiocies. I used to take it that my purpose in life was to eliminate them entirely from my own sphere of influence. You would scarcely credit the pains I used to take to leave no instruction ambiguous, no rules incompatible, no staff unaware of precisely what was expected of them. I wanted to get bureaucracy back its good name, if it ever had one. (I actually suspect that the word was originally coined in a derogatory sense, but I'm always too lazy to look things like that up. Or is it that I can't rid myself of a stupid conviction that it's somehow cheating to look things up instead of knowing them?) I used to be passionate about the virtues of good administration, though. After all, I used to reason, in any tolerably civilized society, it's bureaucracy that makes the world go round. That's why people get so upset by the tiny proportion of cases that show up the inevitable idiocies in any administrative system. Whether they're conscious of it or not, something in them *knows* that the system in question is the very rock on which their houses are built, so to speak, and any minor imperfection in the system becomes an intolerable threat. The administrator, the bureaucrat, must therefore keep striving for absolute perfection. Or so I thought.

Father was always slightly satirical about that. 'Unambiguous instructions?' he said to me one Sunday in the Bold Princess Royal. 'Over there is the most unambiguous instruction you will ever see. Before I finish this port, someone will misunderstand it.' He was right. It was on the door of the gents.

PULL.

Father rarely laughed aloud, but he smiled so much it was hard to know if he was being ironic. Looking back, you could take nearly everything he said in his later years as being ironic. You could certainly take 'My constitutional' as being ironic.

Nowadays I am much more philosophical. Maurice Denby would have smiled at the thought of that. At the irony of it, in fact. Maurice and I were in the same intake in 1946; we were Assistant Prins together in the Private Office for a year. He took early retirement when the chance came up during the Cuts four or five years ago. He was a terrifically bright chap as a young man, third or fourth place in the Civil Service examinations. (I barely scraped in myself.) Great things were expected of Maurice, but he never got beyond Principal. I could have predicted that after working with him a week, but he trusted me and didn't bother to hide himself from me. Maurice was very adept at hiding himself from others when it suited him, as it usually did. I think it took Staff Branch (or Personnel, as they insist on being called nowadays) the better part of two decades to register what I saw more or less straight away, namely that Maurice was not prepared to take on any job that he couldn't do more or less to perfection while firing on three or four cylinders out of six. He was simply not attracted enough by money or status or power to compromise on that point. 'I just cannot see the logic in this theory that one needs to be *extended* by one's work, Grace,' I remember him saying more than once, 'that it is somehow good for the soul to face a constant intellectual challenge. I should've thought that, if one does need such a challenge, and if one cannot find it without having it imposed on one willy-nilly by the job one does for one's bread and butter, then one's intellect is not worth much of a challenge in the first place.'

This is a mere boy of twenty-three or -four speaking. That way of his of talking in measured Mandarin prose certainly did impress (and deceive) a lot of his superiors in those days, but it could also make him sound a pompous prig at times. That was an equally deceptive impression, although a lot of people never saw him otherwise. I think his upbringing must have had a lot to do with it. Maurice comes from an old Catholic family and continues to this day to practise, more or less, the faith of his forefathers. He was privately educated before Oxford, although in a healthy liberal fashion, he always claimed. ('I am quite un-nunstunted, Grace.') His appearance reinforced the impression given by his manner of speaking. He wore a drooping moustache years after it ceased to be fashionable and years before it became fashionable again. (Most of us had seen them only in ancient photographs of our fathers, if not our grandfathers.) When I look at pictures of Maurice taken over a period of the first twenty years or so we knew each other, it is very difficult to detect much change in

185

the man or his clothes. Maurice seemed to have been born middle-aged. His contemporaries spent their time catching up on his maturity until around their fortieth birthdays and thereafter began to envy the effortless way Maurice was keeping his looks and figure.

In those early days in the Private Office, Maurice used to tease me endlessly about my zeal. 'It achieves nothing in the end, Grace, nothing of real moment,' he would assure me, as I faithfully checked and double-checked the facts and arguments in answers to PQs or laboriously translated some working Branch's draft reply to a constituent's letter into English. 'That House is at best a debating society, and what's debate? Oratory, rhetoric, mummery; the mountebank's refuge from rational argument. So why polish, polish, polish, dear girl? What is the point?' My small (and sometimes not so small) explosions of frustration over the inconsistencies and imperceptiveness of our political lords and masters never failed to send Maurice into peals of his silent laughter. (For some reason, laughter stopped Maurice from looking and sounding priggish, only to give him an unmistakable air of guilt. I never spoke to him of this. I no longer remember why.) 'My dear Grace,' he would say, 'you really must not look for consistency in that quarter. What's the point of being powerful if one still has to be consistent? And as for perspicacity, well! Even we can readily see that the issues we are addressing are complex and subtle and not susceptible to simple solutions, but no would-be Government could admit that to the electorate and hope to be returned. To obtain power, a politico either has to believe sincerely that complex matters are straightforward or he has to be capable of pretending convincingly that things are not as they are. A successful politico is either a fool or a rogue, Grace, a fool or a rogue. One simply has to be philosophical about it.' I, of course, knew differently. Ah, the terrible *certainty* of youth.

I no longer recall exactly when my affair with Maurice

Denby began, far less when it finished; we have remained on friendly terms ever since and I saw him in his official capacity almost daily for more than twenty years. It can only have lasted a matter of months at the most. I do remember, though, why it began and ended. It began because Maurice wanted it to. I never understood why, but he wanted it to. Nowadays I am a fat old frump with a caliper and walking-stick, but even forty years ago I was undeniably a frump among frumps. Maurice was the only half-decent offer ever made me. (To be honest, very nearly the only offer at all.) He was perfectly frank with me; he made it quite clear that there was no question of marriage, a far more serious consideration then than now. Marriage was out of the question for Maurice for much the same reason that he eschewed real commitment to his work. He could never bring himself to believe that it was a serious enough thing to deserve his undivided attention. This was actually almost identical to my own lifelong attitude to the same institution. I remember from childhood the words on the label of a matchbox. It read, 'Keep in a dry place and away from children.' Since other children made my childhood more or less a misery and since children in general seem to have been deteriorating ever since, that has always struck me as an admirable precept. The affair ended because I could not convert Maurice to a less philosophical attitude to his career, nor he me to a more philosophical one. As I have said, we remained on perfectly friendly terms.

Years passed. Ever the philosopher, Maurice failed to rise far. More zealously, I rose almost as far as is possible. I expect the shrinks would call it displacement activity on my part, although I have always regarded Freud as utter balls. (Am I entirely alone in finding the smug self-congratulatory old storyteller almost unreadable? The Krauts at least got the storyteller part right when they gave him the Goethe Prize for Literature, but what on *earth* must the competition have been like?) I saw Maurice less and less frequently as time went on. I noticed his health appeared to take a turn for the worse around his fiftieth birthday and he began to look his real age at last, but I never made inquiries. And then, as I have said, he took an early ticket. I never thought to see him more.

And here I am, at the peak of my career and still, as they say, at the height of my powers, happily espousing the philosophical attitude that Maurice Denby urged upon me so often and so glibly all those years ago. I have at long last reached a position where I no longer have to tell myself lies to justify self-interested behaviour, and I find that old Maurice had it almost completely right. I don't let on to my staff, of course. I'm still the Boss Lady to them, the lady who can make things happen. Anything a bit tricky still tends to rise to my exalted level with little more than an endorsement of 'Miss Hewlett?' on it unless they're already sure of my views. (I won't have this 'Ms' thing. I can't say it, and who cares who knows my marital status? In any event, they all call me 'Amazing Grace' behind my back and I let them get on with it. That sort of thing is good for morale.) But nowadays I know what I know.

I should have loved to have said as much to Maurice, but I didn't get the opportunity. I met him by chance walking across St James's Park. Possibly he walks there daily; he's always had a flat in that tall redbrick Vicwardian block on the Pimlico side of Victoria Street. I shouldn't know, as I naturally walk only in emergencies. (Both departmental Rovers had gone sick at the same time.) He had definitely aged since retiring but we recognized each other at once. He immediately starting asking all sorts of questions about the Department and the staff; all pensioners do that given the opportunity, even intelligent ones like Maurice who ought to know better. But then he turned extremely sheepish. 'Look,' he said, 'I really would like to invite you round to the flat some time, but I'm afraid it's impossible.' I made polite noises and would have happily gone on my way, but he wouldn't have it. He suddenly unburdened himself to me; it was as though he had been bottling it up inside for years, never being able to find the words or the occasion before then.

He was married. He couldn't invite anyone around because his wife was not well enough to receive visitors. She had been a chronic invalid most of their married life. (I'm pretty sure Maurice actually started out to say his wife wouldn't *let* him have visitors, but even in a state of agitation he was still able to stop himself in time.) I was almost literally reeling, I can tell you, but there was worse to come. He was not only married; he had been married all the time. Since before we first met, I mean. All during our brief affair, he had had a wife. I felt unable to ask him whether the lady was already an invalid at that remote date. (I wonder why? I should dearly love to know if we were really competing for his favours.) Maurice's official life and, I presume, much or even all his private life had been a tissue of lies for, what? Four decades? It scarcely bears thinking about. My philosophical friend must have been working away far harder all that time at maintaining his fictional persona than ever I did at advancing my own career. *Maurice*, of all people, who so often used to rail at me when I bridled over changing the facts in the interests of the official truth. Frailty, thy name is Legion.

The years fell away from Maurice's face as he poured out his confession to me. It is, as they say, good for the soul. (Had he regularly confessed it to his priest? What would they have given him as penance? Here, too, I felt inexplicably unable to ask.) When he had finally got it all out, he was panting slightly, but he looked as happy as I have ever seen him look. He thanked me for listening. He apologized for any embarrassment caused. He smiled. (Maurice very very rarely smiled.) I began tentatively to ask him the one all-important question not covered by his outpourings, namely, *why*? Why on earth had he started to live this lie in the first place? But he had already started to wish me an over-hearty farewell. He spun on his heel and strode off. I could not tell whether he was consciously ignoring my question or whether the euphoria of his confession genuinely prevented his hearing me. My last sight of him was as he marched away across the bridge over the lake, heedlessly scattering tourists, their children, their breadcrumbs and the birds that they were attempting to feed.

By another of those memorable rather than unusual coincidences, I got home that night to discover that Father's great secret was at last out in the open. Father was very conventional in his dress, with one minor exception. He abominated neckties and avoided wearing one whenever possible. Indoors he usually wore his shirt open at the neck. Outside, he compromised by wearing a cravat, even if he was only going into the garden to write. Father did all his writing in our garden enough for a peacock, sitting on the bench below the black poplar. His smallish name has lasted rather well, by the way. A *Collected Poems* should be out in the spring. But the point I wanted to make was that when he came down that morning, the black tie round that particular neck was enough to dazzle Jane into dumbness. He saw what she was staring at. 'I'm, ah, that is,' he said, 'I mean there's a funeral. Someone has died. You do not know her.' 'Mrs Wilshire?' Jane asked. 'Oh,' he said, 'you did know, then. I often wondered.' And never mentioned the subject again. A fortnight later he was dead himself.

Vanity of vanities, all is vanity. A resonant statement, and a very true one, I always think. But as a statement, it's a failure, isn't it? It fails utterly to convey even a hint of the awful fascination of the vanity.

I look out into our peacock garden and the sparse late-autumn leaves on the poplar over Father's writing bench look more like some disease attacking dead wood than a vital organ of a living tree, but spring will surely come and green the tree once more. Life and death go on. I could watch them forever.